FOLLOW THAT BOY

"You remember I told you," I began hesitantly, "that there was someone else back in Massachusetts. Well, I got a letter from him today. He's saved up enough money to come to Hawaii and visit me. He's coming in two weeks."

Jason said nothing for a moment. "Are you still in love with this guy?"

"I don't know," I said. "I'll have to see him again to find out."

"Oh, sure," Jason said bitterly. "And then we can pick up where we left off, is that what you're saying?"

"Please don't be mad at me," I said in a small voice. "I can't help it that I fell in love with someone before I met you."

Jason didn't stir. He sat like a statue on his motorbike, staring past me. Then he gunned the engine and roared away.

Bantam Sweet Dreams Romances
  by Janet Quin-Harkin
Ask your bookseller for the books you have missed

Follow That Boy

Janet Quin-Harkin

BANTAM BOOKS

RONTO · NEW YORK · LONDON · SYDNEY · AUCKLAND

RL 6, IL age 11 and up

FOLLOW THAT BOY
A Bantam Book / December 1985

Cover photo by Pat Hill

ISBN 0-553-25298-4

Published simultaneously in the United States and Canada

*Bantam Books are published by Bantam Books, Inc. Its trademark,
consisting of the words "Bantam Books" and the portrayal of a
rooster, is Registered in U.S. Patent and Trademark Office and in
other countries. Marca Registrada. Bantam Books, Inc., 666 Fifth
Avenue, New York, New York 10103.*

PRINTED IN THE UNITED STATES OF AMERICA

O   0 9 8 7 6 5 4 3 2 1

Follow That Boy.

Chapter One

"Hi, everybody, I'm home. Wait till you hear my wonderful news!" my father called as he came through the front door and into the living room. I looked up from my homework, Doug from his line of Hot Wheels cars, and Mom came in from the kitchen, where she had been cutting up fresh ginger root. We all took in Dad's bright smile, as well as the pot of red flowers and the bag of goodies he was carrying. Mom eyed him steadily. "So where are we going this time, Walt?" she asked unemotionally.

Dad laughed uneasily. "How did you know it was another transfer?"

Mom wiped her hands on the apron we'd given her on her last birthday that said, "For This I Went To College?" "Walter Johnson," she said,

"I've been married to you for eighteen years. In those eighteen years we've moved eight times. And every single time you've come home to announce another move, you've said exactly the same thing!"

"Really?" Dad looked surprised. "I had no idea."

"And you always bring presents home, too," Doug said eagerly from the floor. "What did you bring this time?"

Dad picked up the plant and held it up for each of us to see. "These flowers," he said dramatically, "are called *Anthuriums*. Here they can only be grown in hot houses, and they cost a fortune. Where we're going they grow wild everywhere. The same goes for the macadamia nuts I happen to have in this bag." He produced them like an eager magician.

"Well," he said, noting our silence. "Doesn't anybody want to know where we're going?"

"From the flowers and nuts, my guess would be Hawaii," Mom said.

Dad's grin broadened. "First try. Very good," he said.

Doug leaped up from the floor, scattering little cars. "Wowee! We're going to Hawaii!" he yelled in a high voice.

Mom smiled too and walked over to Dad. "Hawaii, huh?" she said. "I must say it'll be a nice change from the snow and ice in Birchington." She stood on her toes to give Dad a kiss and took the pot of flowers from him. "These are beautiful, Walt. Imagine being able to grow things like this in the backyard!" she said, carrying the plant into the kitchen as if it were very precious and very fragile.

"Can I try the macca-whatsits nuts?" Doug begged, taking the jar out of Dad's hand.

Curled up in my armchair by the fire, my trigonometry book in my lap, I stared from one member of my family to the next. *Look at them*, a voice screamed inside me. *How can they take it so calmly? They look so pleased with themselves. They don't care that we have to move halfway around the world again!*

I jumped up from my seat, knocking my book to the floor with a crash. Everyone turned to look at me. "I don't understand you!" I yelled. "Do you actually like getting shipped from place to place like an unwanted package? Don't you ever want a real home somewhere? Don't any of you ever want to belong? Well, I do. I want to live somewhere long enough for people to really know me. I don't ever want to keep the walls in my room clean because it's not *really* my room. But none of you care how I feel, do you?" Their mouths opened in astonishment as I pushed past them. I heard Dad shouting my name as I snatched up my parka and ran out the front door and into the freezing night.

The cold wind slapped me in the face, and I pulled the zipper on my coat up a little higher.

Thrusting my hands deep into my pockets, I listened to my feet scrunching on the patches of snow still clinging to the sidewalk. I was only wearing light tennis shoes, so my feet felt cold and wet immediately, but I didn't care. Nobody cared about me, so what did it matter? Let them find my frozen body lying in a ditch somewhere. Then they'd be sorry!

I stomped down the block and turned toward the lights of Main Street. On the way I passed little wooden frame houses with neat, white-fenced front yards and warm, uncomplicated lives going on behind faded drapes. People grew up and died within a few blocks of where they were born. When they went to the store, people asked them about their grandmothers and cousins. In school, teachers remembered that their fathers had played on the football team or that their mothers had been cheerleaders. It was the sort of town where people felt they *belonged*.

But Birchington had a new subdivision out beyond the elementary school. The area was developed to house people like us, people who would live there for only a couple of years while they worked in Boston. It was an easy drive to the city, but far enough away to be full of New England country charm.

For the first time in my life, I had lived in a small town. Usually we lived in large, impersonal suburbs of large, impersonal cities: west of

Houston; just outside Chicago; near Minneapolis; just north of Cincinnati.

My father had selected a house in Birchington because he wanted to please my mother. She'd fallen in love with the town the moment she'd seen it. But all that our living where we did had done, as far as I was concerned, was emphasize how different we were from the people who *really* lived there.

Every move had been hard for me, even though the moves had all been from one tract house to another. All of our houses had had similar floor plans, and all the schools were steel and glass. I still had friends I wrote to from each of those places. But moving to Hawaii was going to be harder than the other moves because I was going to have to leave behind someone who was more than just a friend.

I stepped on a patch of ice, and for a moment I felt myself sliding over the sidewalk, out of control until I steadied myself by grabbing a telephone pole. Slipping reminded me of that afternoon, only three hours earlier, when I'd been at the outdoor skating rink with Don.

"I've decided that I really like winter best," Don had said, skimming to a halt beside me so quickly that the ice flew up in a sparkling spray. He grabbed my hand and started off around the rink, towing me along faster and faster.

"I never used to like winter much," I'd said. "I

always wished I could be like a bear and hibernate."

"But winter is fun," Don said. "You get to have all those great soups and stews and drink hot chocolate—"

"All you think about is food!" I cut in.

"Not true," he said, swinging me around in a circle so that the trees flashed past me in a blur. "I like the clear air and the way the snow sparkles. People have so much energy in winter."

"I know," I said, laughing. "For football and more football." Don had made the varsity team that year, and I had sat huddled under blankets through every game, cheering wildly.

"For other things besides football," he said, giving me a knowing look. His dark eyes usually sparkled when he smiled, but in the brilliant afternoon sunlight, they had positively flashed. I couldn't get over how handsome he was. It was hard to believe that he was really my boyfriend.

In fact, at the beginning of the year I wondered if I'd ever find a boyfriend. My girlfriends were always telling me I was pretty and that they wished they could be tall and slim like me, but I thought I was *too* thin. Pants always slid down on my nonexistent hips. I didn't like my hair much either. It was fine and flyaway and an uninspired ash blond. But I had blue-green eyes that slanted up just a little at the corners and a fairly nice-looking nose. Also my body was in good shape because I played a lot of sports. The trouble was that, in spite of my looks, I wasn't one of those girls who made heads turn as she walked down the hall. And it usually took me a long time to get to know people well, and by then we were moving again.

But when we moved to Massachusetts, things were miraculously different. My high school was very small. When there are only three hundred and fifty kids in an entire school, it's easy to get to know people. Also it was a school that was proud of its championship girls' soccer team, and I had played a lot of soccer in Houston, the last place we'd lived. It just happened that the most popular girls in the school also played soccer. One of them, Dee Dee Hunt, invited me to a party at her house at the beginning of the year. That's where I met Don. It was like one of those sentimental old movies—eyes meeting across a crowded room, romantic music playing. I could tell that he had noticed me, and I was desperate to find an excuse to talk to him.

Then a small miracle happened. Dee Dee played games at her party. She had us passing oranges under our chins and matchboxes on our noses. Don was next to me for the matchbox on the nose race. And there was no way he could make the box stay on my ridiculously little nose. It just refused. Don's elegant, streamlined nose held it perfectly still while he stood, looking down at me with those perfect dark eyes fringed by incredibly thick lashes. Patiently, he tried to pass the matchbox on to me. I was so nervous at being that close to a gorgeous boy that I did what I always do when I'm nervous, I started to giggle. My whole body shook with laughter.

"I'm sorry," I said between giggles. "I can't help myself. It's just so ridiculous."

"I know," he said, his voice deep and smooth. "Just hold still, and we'll get it." He grasped my shoulders and held me tightly, his face only inches away from mine. I could hardly breathe.

"I'm sorry," I said as the box fell to the floor. "I just don't seem to have the right kind of nose."

"You have an adorable little nose," he said, touching it lightly with his finger. "They just don't have the right kind of matchbox." Then he flashed me a heart-stopping smile. "I'm Don Partridge," he said. "And I don't know you, which is crazy, because I thought I knew everyone in this school."

"I'm Kristy Johnson," I said. "And I just moved here a couple of months ago."

Then he'd taken me out to the barbecue table to get something to eat, and by the time we'd done the next relay, passing Life Savers on toothpicks held in our teeth, I was hopelessly in love with him. He drove me home that night, and I had seen him every day since. It was a perfect relationship. He was funny and smart, a great football player, and my family liked him. I had daydreamed of going to his senior prom, wearing a long white dress, flowers entwined in my hair.

I had seen a dress like it in the window of McGregor's Department Store a few days before. Now, I walked down Main Street to the store. As I stood looking at the dress, I thought about the fact that I wouldn't be there for the prom. Maybe Don would take another girl in that same dress. Maybe he'd have forgotten all about me by then.

"It's just not fair," I muttered as I started walking again, striding past the drugstore and the corner grocery and O'Brien's Hardware and Nancy's Yarns. "I have the right to a life, too. I'm not just a piece of furniture they can keep crating up and shipping off to new places. I'm old enough to have a say in things now. I'm going to go back home and tell them that I'm not moving, and that's that!"

Chapter Two

My parents were very nice to me when I got home. They smiled and said they understood how I felt. But I knew they didn't. When we moved, my father always had a promotion and a new challenge at work. My mother kept herself busy by taking classes at local colleges. Wherever we went, she'd sign up right away for classes—making stained glass, painting with watercolors, restoring antiques, or gourmet cooking. It didn't seem to matter to her what town she was in as long as there was a college nearby. As for my little brother, he's one of those lucky people who makes friends instantly. The moment we arrived in a new town, Doug would get on his bike and ride around the neighborhood. Within two days he could tell us who lived in every house

10

and how many children and pets they had. Everyone liked Doug. He'd be an instant hit in Hawaii, just the way he'd been everywhere else. So how could any of them understand me? How could they understand that for the first time in my life I'd really begun to belong somewhere?

Being Don's girlfriend had opened up a wonderful new world for me. Don had three sisters and two brothers as well as hundreds of cousins. He seemed to be related to most of the town. There was the Partridge Bakery and Partridge Shell Station, both owned by distant relatives of his. There was even a Partridge on the town council. Don took me with him when he went to visit his grandmother in the old three-story brick house behind the park. She baked all her own bread and had made quilts for every bed in the house, including the big four-poster where Don's father had been born. Being in that house was like stepping into a historical TV program.

Don's family was always having big gatherings, too. Every birth, death, marriage, and graduation was an excuse to put up trestle tables in his grandmother's backyard and pile them high with food. After they got to know me, I was included a couple of times, and it was wonderful to sit right in the middle of them, everyone yelling and laughing at once. Then they'd fall quiet to listen to uncle Joseph talk about the big snowstorm of 1922 or the day the courthouse caught fire when he was a boy. They talked confidently about the future, too—about when the big pasture over beyond the bridge would be sold to a shopping center developer and how that would affect the stores on Main Street, or whether young Annie would ever marry that Thomas boy and settle down in the apartment above the store. They all took it for granted that life would continue, pretty much unchanged, for the rest of their lives. And once I had had a taste of that sort of life, I didn't want to give it up.

"It's easy for all of you," I reasoned as my mother put a plate of steaming ginger chicken in front of me. "Birchington doesn't mean any more to you than any of the other places we've lived. But I've made friends here—special friends—"

They knew I meant Don. I saw my mother glance over at my father.

"Don's your first real boyfriend, darling," she said. "So naturally he's very special to you. I know you don't want to leave him, and I know it seems like the end of the world right now. But believe me, you'll have lots of other boyfriends. I'll bet there are plenty of terrific boys in Hawaii."

"It wouldn't be the same," I said angrily. "It's different with Don and me. We're just right for each other. We wouldn't want to date anyone else, ever."

"Then maybe it's a good idea that we're moving," my father said firmly. "I certainly don't want you getting too serious with any one boy at your age. You're only sixteen, Kristy, much too young to tie yourself down to one boy."

I jumped up from the table, feeling angry and confused. I felt as if they were all suddenly against me. "I bet you engineered this whole thing, didn't you?" I started to yell at my father. "The moment you saw that I had actually managed to get myself a real boyfriend, like any normal girl, you panicked. I bet you asked to be transferred again because you didn't want me to have a normal life. No, you want me to be trapped with you and float off to a new place every two years. I'll never get a chance to have real friends." Then I turned and ran upstairs to my room.

I lay on my bed in the darkness, watching the shadows of bare-branched trees dance on my wall. Tears trickled down my cheeks and dropped onto the pillow below me. I really wanted to phone Don, but the only phone was in the living room. I certainly wasn't going to talk to him right under their noses. I felt as if I'd burst with anger and helplessness and despair. Finally I must have drifted off to sleep.

When I woke up the next morning, my eyelids were puffy, and my eyes were red and had dark circles under them.

One look at your face and Don will be glad you're going, I thought, splashing cold water on my face. Then I put on a base coat of makeup and some blusher. I added lots of eye shadow and liner around my eyes. My parents didn't really approve of makeup, so I had to sneak out without breakfast. I felt so hungry on the way to school that I had to stop off at Sarah Jane's Coffee Shop for a doughnut.

"My, but don't you look grown-up," Sarah Jane said from behind the counter. "Don's going to think he's going out with a grown woman!" I couldn't tell if she approved or not. That was one thing about people from New England—I never knew what they were feeling.

I hung around Don's locker, hoping I'd see him before class. But the first people I saw were Dee Dee and her gang. They also noticed the makeup.

"Hey, it's the new, improved Kristy Johnson," Dee Dee said, eyeing me closely. Again I couldn't tell whether it was with approval or not. "You've never worn makeup before. Why the sudden change?"

"It's not a permanent change," I said. "I was crying last night and my face was a mess this morning, that's all."

"It looks good on you," Robin said. "Makes you look much older."

"What were you upset about?" Dee Dee asked with concern. "Did you and Don have a fight?"

"Much worse than that," I said, brushing my hair back from my face and giving a big sigh. "My family is being transferred again—"

"But you only just got here in August," Anita interrupted.

"I know it," I said in frustration. "That's the

14

story of my life. As soon as we arrive and settle in, we move again."

"Why do you move so much? Is your dad with the military?" Charlene asked.

"He computerizes companies," I said. "He studies them and then sets up computer systems for them. Then when he gets the system going, he moves on."

"What a bummer," Patti said. "I'd hate that."

"I hate it, too," I said. "But especially this time—"

"Why, where're you going?" Anita asked.

"Hawaii!"

They all burst out talking at the same time. "Oh, yeah—Hawaii, that sounds like a real pain. Oh, poor Kristy. Imagine—boring old Hawaii—all those cute guys with tans and surfboards!"

"You don't want to go to Hawaii?" Robin asked, her blue eyes opening very wide.

"I don't want to go anywhere," I said. "I like it here."

"But all those tan guys with the sun-bleached hair?"

"You're forgetting about Don," I said. "I don't want to leave him."

"Tell you what," Dee Dee said, laughing. "Why don't we trade places. You stay here with my family, and I'll go to Hawaii for you!"

Then the bell rang, and they all headed for class. I stood there, thinking. One part of Dee Dee's idea seemed wonderful, the perfect answer to everything. I'd just stay with Dee Dee's family, and she could go to Hawaii. I knew it would never work, but it was fun to think about.

At lunchtime Don was waiting for me outside my English class. "What's going on?" he asked me. "There's a rumor going around school that you're leaving."

"My family's being transferred again," I said. "To Hawaii."

"Already?" he said. "But I thought you were going to be here for two years at least. Oh, Kristy, I don't want you to go." He paused and then went on. "But if you have to go, I guess Hawaii is better than most places. Like a permanent vacation."

"Who wants to live in the middle of a bunch of tourist hotels and crowded beaches?" I said. "What else is there in Hawaii? Natives living in palm huts? We'll probably have to live in a hut, too."

"Oh, sure," Don said, laughing. "And spear fish in the lagoon for breakfast! It's not going to be that bad, Kristy."

"But it is," I said. "I don't want to leave Birchington. I like it here—and I don't want to leave you."

Don took me into his arms, right there in the hall. "We'll find a way, Kristy," he said. "If you don't want to go, you shouldn't have to. Tell them that psychologists have proven it's harmful to move a kid in the middle of high school. At the very least, they should let you stay here till the end of the school year."

"Yeah," I said, feeling hopeful for the first time. "Maybe they'd let me stay on until the end of the school year." That meant Don's senior prom, all the graduation parties, all the things I'd dreamed of. After that, Don would be away at college, and it wouldn't be so hard to leave.

"But where would you stay?" he asked, putting an arm around my shoulder as we walked to class together.

"Dee Dee wants to go instead of me," I said and laughed. "I'll just stay with her family."

Don turned and smiled at me. He was normally very serious looking, but when he smiled, his whole face lit up. "Don't worry," he said. "We'll figure something out."

Later in the day I sat next to Dee Dee in chorus. "You look much better," she said. "This morning you looked as if you were about to burst into tears any second."

"Well, Don and I talked," I said. "And we're determined to find a way for me to stay here, at least for a while."

The choir master tapped his baton to call us to attention, and we began to sing:

"I must away, I cannot stay,
I'm leaving my true love today . . ."

Chapter Three

"It'll be OK, you'll see," Don said as we walked home together. It was very cold, but I could feel the warmth of his arm around me.

"How?" I asked bleakly, Despite that afternoon's recovery, I just couldn't think of a way to work things out.

He stared ahead with his serious, thoughtful look. "Maybe we could find you an apartment to rent."

"I don't think my parents would ever go along with that," I said. I was thinking more that I could never go along with that. My mother was such a fabulous cook that I hadn't even learned how to boil an egg. I pictured myself sitting in a cold, bare room, reading the directions on a can of baked beans before I heated them.

"Then I'll ask my parents," Don said. "Maybe I can persuade them to let you live with us."

"But you don't have any room at your house," I said.

Don gave me one of his teasing looks. "My bedroom's very big," he said.

I had to smile. "My mom and dad certainly wouldn't go along with that," I said.

"Spoilsports," Don said, giving my arm an extra squeeze. "Hey, maybe we can move that old sofa bed from the basement into Dad's study."

"But he does his accounts in there," I said. "He wouldn't want a strange girl keeping her things there."

"You're not a strange girl," Don said. "You're almost like family, and family always help one another out."

I began to feel hopeful again. We stopped off at Don's house, and Don carefully brought the subject up with his mother. His mother was very sympathetic.

"It's certainly not fair to move poor Kristy so far away in the middle of the school year," she said. "Let's give it some thought, shall we? Maybe Aunt Mabel wouldn't mind having her. And Grandma's got all that space. She's getting old, though." Mrs. Partridge's thoughts seemed to wander for a moment before she said firmly, "But I'm sure we can come up with something!"

"Well, you look much happier," my mother

said when I burst into the kitchen at dinner time. "We were very worried about you. I thought we'd have you nursing a broken heart for months! Here," she said, "have a scone and some jam; they're delicious. This Englishwoman in my cooking class showed me how to make them."

I put butter and jam on one and bit into it. It was heavenly. I finished it and I picked up another one to butter. I'm one of those lucky people who can eat and eat and never gain a pound.

"I think I've managed to sort things out," I said, taking a bite of the scone. "Don and I both agree that it isn't fair to make me move before the end of the school year, so Don's family is going to arrange for me to live with them. Isn't that wonderful? Then I can fly out to Hawaii at the beginning of the summer."

For a long moment my mother didn't say anything. I could hear the clock ticking, the vegetables bubbling on the stove, and my brother singing tunelessly to himself as he played with his cars in the living room. Then my mother said, "So you've managed to work everything out without us. Is that right?"

"I guess so," I said nervously.

"And that's what you really want, is it? To stay with some boy you only met a few months ago and leave your family?"

I laughed hesitantly. "Oh, come on, Mom. You make it sound like I'm about to run off and elope with him. It's just for a few months, just till the end of the school year."

"And did it never occur to you," my mother said in a voice that was not much more than a whisper, "that your family needs you, that we need your support?"

"That's ridiculous," I snapped. "You've never needed me. Dad charges around being efficient, and you'll instantly sign up for hula classes and three hundred ways to roast a suckling pig, and Doug will speak Hawaiian fluently by the end of the first week. I'll be the only one who doesn't fit in there." I stalked out of the kitchen with tears in my eyes.

Later that evening I heard Dad and Mom talking. I was on my way into the kitchen to get some and saw them sitting together by the fire, talking in low voices. They didn't notice me.

"So she announced it just like that?" my father was saying.

"She said she'd worked it all out!"

"Well, at least that proves that she's finally growing up and trying to stand on her own feet," Dad said. "I suppose that's a good thing. But she couldn't seriously think that we'd let her stay with her boyfriend for six months?"

My mother sighed. "I suppose we must be old-fashioned, Walt," she said.

"Old-fashioned or not, I set standards for my family and I expect my family to follow them," my father blustered, his voice rising.

I couldn't stand it any longer. Stepping out of the shadows, I said angrily, "It's not like that at all. You make it sound terrible that I want to stay with Don. It's just that we want to be together a little while longer. He's going to arrange for me to live with an aunt or another relative, that's all."

My father's face was bright red. "He's not going to arrange anything at all," he said. "Because you're coming with us. We're a family, young lady, and a family sticks together. The only reason we've survived living in all the places we have is that we have each other. The company said I could have a few weeks to wrap things up here, but I don't think we want to drag this out any longer than we have to. I'll phone Phillips in Honolulu and have him rent an apartment for us right away. In fact, that's even better. It will be the Christmas break, so neither you nor your brother will miss any school."

After that there didn't seem to be anything I could do. I thought about running away or hiding out in somebody's attic until my parents had left, but I didn't have the nerve to do that. After all, they *were* my family, and I did love them—in spite of the way they were breaking my heart.

"I'll write to you often," Don said. "I can do it in economics—that class is so boring! I'll try and phone you as often as I can, too. And I'll save the money I make working at my uncle's gas station on weekends. Maybe I'll even be able to afford to fly out next summer. OK?"

"OK," I said, managing a very weak smile. "But what about your prom—you'll have to take some-one else to your senior prom!"

He smiled. "Then start saving your money, and you can fly back for it."

"I'll try," I said hesitantly. "But I don't think I'd be very good at picking pineapples or cutting sugarcane."

"You make it sound like you're going to some secluded island," he said, laughing.

"That's how it is," I said. "There are hotels all along the beach, and nothing but pineapples growing behind them."

"I think you're in for a shock," Don said. "I've heard it's pretty civilized there."

"I hope so. I really don't want to live in a grass shack."

He shook his head. "You're funny," he said. "And I'm going to miss you."

The days seemed to fly by. I watched with a sinking feeling as my favorite possessions disappeared into boxes. Finally the house was just an empty shell, nothing left as evidence of the family that had lived there.

I realized with a horrible jolt that we would actually be leaving for Hawaii the next day. Walking down Main Street, I tried to take in every detail. The doughnut shop, the little, wood-framed library, Don's grandmother's house with smoke curling up from the chimney, even the icicles hanging from the bandstand in the park—all of it was so familiar and so perfect.

I was dreading that last evening with Don. It was going to be so hard, and I was afraid that I might break down and cry like an idiot.

"Do you want to go for a walk?" I asked him when he showed up just as we were finishing dinner. "We can't really stay here. There's nowhere to sit, and nothing to drink, and no TV."

"Sounds like a really fun place," Don said, laughing. "Anyway, I don't want to just hang around tonight. I want you to have happy memories. I've got the evening all planned. Now, come on, get your coat!"

We drove across town in his father's big old truck.

"Where're we going?" I asked.

"You'll see," Don said, giving me a mysterious smile. "As a matter of fact, I'm planning to kidnap you and keep you hidden in the forest until your parents leave!"

"What a terrific idea," I said, laughing. "Right now I'd do anything not to go! Where were you planning on keeping me?"

"In a little hut up in the woods," he said, still smiling. "Of course, it has no heat, and bears use it occasionally. But I'm sure you'll be comfortable."

I snuggled up against him, feeling the warmth

24

of his arm through his jacket. "Anything to be close to you," I said.

He brought the truck to a halt. "Oh, Kristy, don't," he said in a choked voice. "I can't bear to think that you're really going tomorrow. I'm going to miss you so much."

"I don't know how I'm going to get along without you," Don said. "I've left a lot of places before, but saying goodbye never hurt this much."

He slid his arm around me and drew me close to him. "We'll find a way to get back together," he said. "Even if I have to go to the University of Hawaii and study hula dancing."

"Oh, Don," I whispered, "I'll never love anyone the way I love you. I'll think about you every minute."

I was stopped from saying any more by Don's lips. They met mine in a warm, tender kiss. I closed my eyes and found myself thinking, *I must remember every detail of this moment, so I can think about it when I'm feeling really lonely and sad.*

"I hope you'll remember what a good kisser I am," Don said, making me wonder if he could read my thoughts.

I managed to laugh. "I'll tell everyone I meet in Hawaii. I'll say, 'You should go to Birchington, Mass., and visit Don Partridge if you want to meet a really good kisser!' "

"No way," he said. "My lips are reserved for one person!"

Suddenly he looked at his watch, holding it up to the light of the street lamp. "Hey, we'd better get going, or they'll wonder what happened to us!" he said.

"Get going where?" I asked. Again he smiled secretively and we drove on. Then, at last, we turned off the main highway onto a dirt road, bumping and crunching over the packed snow.

"Isn't this Dee Dee's house?" I asked.

"Could be," he said, pulling up beside the barn that was on her property. "We decided you'd be very depressed on your last night here, so we planned a little celebration."

I looked out, and there hanging across Dee Dee's front porch was a big painted sign, "We'll Miss You, Kristy!"

At that moment I couldn't stop my tears. "Hey," Don said, putting his arms around me. "I brought you here because I didn't want you to cry."

"It's just so good to know that people care about me here," I said, giving a big sniff.

"Why wouldn't they care about you? I mean, anyone who has such a cute little nose can't help but have lots of friends," Don said, giving me a kiss. Then we got out and walked toward the house.

Inside, a huge group of kids yelled "Surprise!" Then they clustered around me talking, laughing, and joking.

The party couldn't have been better. Of course

Don was the chief planner, so we had all the things I liked to eat and drink—things like baked potatoes with sour cream and bacon, and hot chocolate with whipped cream and cinnamon. And we played charades and laughed ourselves silly.

After a late supper, the mood quieted down. Kids lay around, listening to music and talking in low voices. A big white winter moon was shining in through the window.

"You want to take a little walk?" Don asked me. "We won't have much time alone together."

We slipped out into a moonlit garden. We could see for miles across the rolling countryside—the smooth white fields and the dark woodland shapes peeping out from under blankets of snow. There was no wind, and even though our breath rose in steamy clouds, it didn't feel cold. Maybe that was because Don was so close beside me.

"Doesn't it feel like we're the only people in the whole world, Kristy?" he asked, holding me close to him.

"I wish we were," I whispered back. "Then nobody could drag me to Hawaii."

"Only happy thoughts tonight!" Don cut in. "No tears allowed. Come on, give me a kiss."

"Your nose is cold," I said, drawing back laughing.

"So is yours," he said. "Don't the Eskimos kiss by rubbing noses?"

We were standing there laughing, kissing, and rubbing noses when there was a noise behind us.

"There they are! They thought they could ditch us, but they were wrong!" Light streamed out of the open kitchen door. Suddenly something whizzed through the air and splattered against my side. A great whoop of delight went up.

"Come on, let's get them!" someone else yelled.

"This is war," Don shouted back, already bending to scoop up some snow. After that things were pretty confused. Snow was flying in all directions. Everybody was screaming and laughing, and by the time we finished, we were all wet and snowy.

"I'd better take Kristy home before she catches pneumonia," Don said. "She's got a long day tomorrow."

I said my goodbyes, then Don and I climbed back into the truck. Everyone stood in the yard, waving. Don and I drove home without talking, sitting so close that we must have looked to an outsider like a two-headed person.

I replayed the party over and over in my mind as we drove to the airport the next morning. Dad had arranged for a furnished apartment for us because our own furniture was being shipped by sea and wouldn't arrive for three months. We packed just our summer clothes, and the rest was being sent with the furniture. I didn't even bring my collection of china animals.

I didn't say a word all the way to the airport. Watching the snow-covered countryside flash past, I thought about how I'd miss the way the trees sparkled under fluffy white cloaks and the houses nestled under their white roof-blankets. The whole world seemed so clean and crisp. *And to think that I didn't even like winter before I met Don*, I thought gloomily. *I won't have a chance to go skiing now or on a sleigh ride. Nothing will be fun anymore.*

I also didn't say a word on the flight to San Francisco. Mom asked me a couple of times if I was feeling all right, but I just grunted. I wanted them to know how much I was suffering and that it was all their fault. We waited at the San Francisco airport for a couple of hours, feeling tired and bad tempered. Then at seven o'clock we boarded the plane for Hawaii. We must have been the only nontourists on the plane. Everyone was dressed in Hawaiian shirts or muumuus. They carried straw hats and beach rolls and were all talking and laughing loudly. I felt very out of place in my sweat shirt and jeans. My sweat shirt said HAAVAHD. Don had bought it for me as a going-away present. I was determined to wear it forever to let everyone know that my heart was still on the East Coast.

Even the flight attendants wore Hawaiian shirts as they handed out pineapple juice and packages of macadamia nuts. I began to wonder if this was the standard food in Hawaii. Would I be taking a macadamia-nut butter and jelly sandwich to school from now on? The plane took off, and I looked down to see San Francisco lying like a string of jewels along the blackness of its bay. I watched it disappear behind the wing. My last link with the mainland slipped away until it faded into blackness.

Chapter Four

The first thing that I noticed about Hawaii was the smell. As we came out of the airport into the soft, dark night, the scent of tropical flowers overpowered me. Hundreds of them must have been blooming unseen around me.

"Doesn't it smell lovely," my mother said, taking a deep breath.

"They probably planted flowers all around the airport to hide the smell of the fumes," I said, walking ahead of her to the palm-lined pick-up zone. Dad waved for a cab, and an old Buick screeched to a halt in front of us. An enormous brown-skinned man got out. He must have been six feet tall and nearly as wide, and he had a face like a boxer after too many fights.

"Which hotel, folks?" he asked in a deep, rumbling voice.

"We're not going to a hotel," my father said. "We'd like to go to the Lanai Apartments."

As he put our suitcases into the trunk of the car, he asked, "Is that over by the canal?" He seemed puzzled.

"I think so," my father said. "Here's the address."

The man read the address on the piece of paper my father was holding. "That's right," he said. "Over by the canal. OK, jump in. Let's get going." He held the doors for us, and my father got into the front passenger seat while Mom, Doug, and I sat in back with the luggage.

"So how come you're not staying in a hotel?" he questioned as we drove off.

"We've come to live here," my brother said.

"Is that right?" The big man chuckled. "Well, isn't that wonderful. Welcome to Hawaii. You sure chose the right place to live. God's own country here."

Then he spent the rest of the trip asking us questions and pointing out the sights as we passed them. There wasn't much to see on the way into town, though. Mostly we drove past pineapple factories, and the smell of pineapple was very strong through the open windows.

"You see," I said triumphantly. "Only the airport smells good. The rest of the place stinks of pineapple."

"Sorry about that, folks," the driver said, turning around to talk to me while the car wandered all over the road. "But I have to keep the windows down. The air conditioner doesn't work."

Soon the factories gave way to modern apartment buildings, and at last we pulled up in front of a high-rise building, set amid other high rises.

"Here we are, folks," the driver said. "Lanai Apartments." He unloaded the bags and then refused to take a tip. "That's my welcome-to-the-Islands present," he said, grinning broadly. And he got back into the car and roared away.

The apartment was on the fifth floor and it was furnished very simply with rattan furniture. The floors were bare. In the dark it was hard to see much of the view from my bedoom window, but I could see the canal and lights on in some high-rise buildings. I lay in the unfamiliar bed, too tired to sleep. I heard voices coming from neighbors' balconies, which Dad said were called *lanais* here. The voices sounded loud and shrill and were accompanied with a lot of laughter. A guitar was strumming somewhere, and people started singing. I wondered how everyone could be so cheerful in the middle of the night. Then I remembered the time difference—it was only nine o'clock in Hawaii, but it was two o'clock in the morning to us!

Finally I drifted off to sleep and woke the next

morning to brilliant sun streaming in my window. Doug came bounding in, looking wide-awake and full of energy. "Wow, you should see it out there, Kristy. It's just like summer. Will you walk down to the beach with me?"

"Go away," I growled. "Why do you always have so much energy?"

"Oh, come on. Get up, lazybones," he said, grabbing at the covers. I chased him away, but by then I was fully awake anyway, so I walked over to the window to look at the canal. The canal was a bright and shimmering straight line, and a huge golf course ran along one side of it. Behind the golf course there were more high-rise buildings and then mountains beyond them. The mountains were covered in shaggy green, and clouds floated beside them. As I watched, the clouds parted to reveal a steep valley with a rainbow stretched across it. It was the most dramatic landscape I'd ever seen. I half expected to see an enchanted castle perched on a cliff with Prince Charming riding up to it!

Mom and Dad were still sleeping, and Doug and I were starving. "Let's go and see if there's a doughnut shop here," Doug suggested.

"That's a good idea," I said.

"I'm wearing my bathing suit, just in case," Doug said. "Are you?"

"No," I said. "I just want to get doughnuts and come back. I'm not too wild about oceans."

We went outside into the heat. Even though it

34

was early in the morning, it was very hot. I realized that my lightest summer clothes were not going to be light enough. I wished that I'd put on my one pair of shorts, but I didn't have the energy to go back upstairs and get them. An enormous old woman in a flowered muumuu was shepherding two tiny brown children out the front door. They were both yelling something at the same time while she said, "You two just mind your *tutu* now!"

I began to feel as if I were living in a foreign country. The whole place seemed to be populated by brown-skinned giants who didn't speak English. We turned the corner at the end of the block and headed away from the canal, toward the towering hotels. Everyone we passed on the sidewalk was walking slowly, as if they could spend all day enjoying the sunshine. Everyone wore thongs, and you could hear the rhythmic flop-flopping as they passed by. In between the high rises were scattered old wooden houses with palm trees in front of them. Their yards were filled with blossoms, and the strong scent stayed with us well down the block.

As soon as we turned off the sleepy side street onto the main drag, everything was bustle and business. On one side of the street, hotels were lined up side by side, hiding the view of the ocean. The other side of the street was made up mostly of restaurants and souvenir shops. The stores all displayed the same items—printed fabric, beach wear, straw hats and bags, monkeys carved from coconuts, and shell necklaces.

"The beach must be somewhere nearby," Doug said.

"You're not going swimming without Mom and Dad," I said firmly. "I don't want to have to drag you out from under those big waves."

Doug laughed. "You couldn't save a flea," he said. "You can't even swim."

"I can, too," I spat back.

"Well, only just," he said. "You never learned to put your face in the water, remember?"

"That's because the water was so cold," I said, defending myself. "I could swim if I had to."

To keep Doug quiet we walked through one of the hotels to take a look at the beach. It was full of perfect, tan bodies. There was not one person who looked as sickly and pale as I did.

I dragged Doug away from the beach, and we started looking for a doughnut shop again. After we didn't find one in four blocks, we settled for danishes at Jack-in-the-Box and brought a couple back for Mom and Dad.

"You see," I said triumphantly to my brother as we turned toward the apartment, "I knew this place wasn't civilized. They don't even have any doughnut shops."

"They have a Jack-in-the-Box," Doug said. "And a beach."

"I can't survive without my morning doughnut," I said.

"You're an old grouch," Doug commented, running on ahead of me.

I walked slowly behind him, not attempting to catch up even though I knew that an eight-year-old boy shouldn't be allowed to run alone through a strange city. All I could think of was the doughnut shop at home. We always met there after soccer games and football games and early-morning practices. Now there'd be no more doughnuts. I couldn't even explain that to Doug. He wouldn't understand that a doughnut had suddenly become the symbol of everything I had left behind.

Chapter Five

Mom and Dad were thankful for the pastries.
Looking very pale and tired, they sat down to eat
them. Mom said she had a headache and was
going to take it easy. Doug bullied Dad into taking him for a swim. That left just me.

"Why don't you find out where the closest
supermarket is so that I can go buy food later?"
Mom suggested. "That would be a real help,
Kristy."

The heat was already beginning to get to me,
and I really didn't feel like going outside again.
But I didn't want to stay in doing nothing either.
So I changed into shorts—even though I shuddered at the thought of people seeing my white
skin—and a halter top and took some money to

buy sunglasses. If the sun really shined as much as they said it did, I'd go crazy from squinting.

I left the apartment and walked to the elevator. A pretty Chinese girl about my age was standing there. She was wearing a gorgeous pair of peacock blue shorts and a matching bikini top, which emphasized the golden bronze of her skin. I felt ugly with my pale, white skin. Her face lit up when she saw me.

"Hey, you must have just moved into number fifty-two," she said. "How do you like Hawaii?"

"I'm still getting over jet lag," I said. "Ask me next week and I'll tell you."

She laughed musically. "Where are you from?"

"We've just moved from near Boston, but I was born in Pennsylvania."

We continued talking as the elevator arrived and we got in.

"What's it like there?" she asked. "Pretty cold right now, huh?"

"There's two feet of snow in Boston."

She shuddered. "How terrible. I bet you couldn't wait to get away?"

Not wanting to answer this, I asked instead, "Where are you from?"

She looked surprised, then let out another laugh. "From right here, Hawaii. Where'd you think?"

"I don't know," I said, seeing her amused face looking at me with interest. "I thought you came from China or somewhere."

She laughed as if I'd said something funny. "My ancestors came from China, way back," she said. "Or at least some of them did. My grandma was pure Hawaiian, and I think there was someone Japanese, too. I'm a proper Hawaiian chop suey," she said, "like most people on these islands. My name's Ellen, by the way. Ellen Chan. What's yours?"

"Kristy Johnson," I said.

"Nice to meet you, Kristy," she said. "Listen, I've got to go, or I'll be late for work. I help out at my dad's store during vacations, and he'll kill me if I'm late again. But I'll see you around, OK? Bye, Kristy—have fun. By the way, if you're going to the beach, don't forget to put on suntan oil, or you'll burn that mainland skin!"

She left me in the entrance to the building, and I walked down the block slowly, feeling the sweat run down between my shoulder blades. I found a supermarket not too far away and bought myself a Popsicle. Then I wandered on down to the main street again. Little stalls had opened up along the whole block, selling everything from T-shirts to gold chains. The stall vendors called out to me as I went past, "Just what you need, miss—nice straw hat to keep off the sun. Stop you getting freckles. Genuine opal rings. Just take a look. Here, try this one on."

In addition to the stall vendors, men walked up and down the sidewalk waving brochures at everyone who passed. "Sunset cruise tonight.

Free dinner. Hula show. Bargain tickets." My head began to spin, and I slipped into the big air-conditioned shopping center to get away from the heat and noise. I noticed with amazement that they were all decorated for Christmas. I had almost forgotten that it was only eight days away.

Down on the ground floor a Santa was walking around handing out candy canes and announcing that you could have your picture taken with him at two o'clock. He was also reminding people that the hula show was about to start.

A crowd was gathering around a platform, and I joined them. Then there was a furious beating of drums, and six girls rushed onto the make-shift stage, rustling as they walked. The music started, and at first I thought I was seeing things. They weren't playing Hawaiian music at all, and the girls were wearing red tinsel skirts and gold tinsel leis round their necks. They were dancing a slow hula to the song "White Christmas." It was all so commercial and phony. I turned and pushed my way out through the crowd before the number ended.

This is going to be like living in the middle of Disneyland, I thought angrily as I stepped out into the heat again. My wind wandered back to Main Street in Birchington, Massachusetts. Two strings of colored Christmas lights, which stretched between the post office and the police department, and a Christmas tree outside the library were the town's only decorations. There was no need for fake snow. It lay naturally on window ledges and roofs. There was no need for phoniness there. It was a real town full of real people. And now it was six thousand miles away. I imagined Don and his friends getting together for holiday parties. "What happened to Kristy?" they'd ask. "Hey, think about Kristy lying on a beach, lucky creep," they'd say. Then soon, I wouldn't even come up in conversation anymore.

I was just about to cross the street when I heard the furious jangling of a bell, and a bicycle came straight at me. I threw myself out of its path into a tub of flowers.

"Hey, are you all right?" the bicycle's owner asked, leaping down to help me out of the flowers.

I lay there with my legs sticking up, helpless, and I started to giggle.

"Here, give me your hand," the boy said, dragging me to my feet again. I picked myself up, still giggling, and noticed that I had crushed a few branches.

"I hope they don't put me in jail for destroying public property," I said.

"Oh, they'll give you at least ten years for destroying plants as rare as those," the boy said. I looked up at him and found myself staring into a face like the one my friends had talked about. The boy facing me had tanned skin, a slightly peeling nose, bright blue eyes, and sun-bleached hair. He grinned at me reassuringly. "Don't worry, those things grow like weeds. I'm only glad I didn't cause a worse accident with this monster machine. They aren't very easy to control."

Then I examined the bicycle carefully and found it had two wheels at the back and a bench seat behind the driver.

"What a weird, er—" I started. "What is it?"

His eyebrows shot up. "You must be new to the Islands," he said. "This is the main form of tourist transport around here. It's a pedicab. This one belongs to my friend. He's sick today and begged me to take it out and work for him. He's saving madly to get to the mainland."

"Sensible boy," I said.

The boy looked at me with interest. "You don't like it here?" he asked.

I shrugged my shoulders. "I guess it's fine for a vacation," I said. "But not if you have to live here. It's so phony—all this tourist junk and the fake grass skirts. And the Hawaiians—I don't think anyone would want to put up with them for long. They could drive you crazy."

"Oh, why is that?" he asked, grinning at me.

I grinned back. He had such a friendly, open face. I couldn't believe my luck. I had met a fellow outsider, someone I could talk to openly. "They're so noisy," I said. "They honk their horns when they drive, and they seem to talk and laugh nonstop, and when they aren't talking and laughing, they're singing."

The boy went on smiling. "Is that so bad?" he asked.

"Sure it is. I like the peace and quiet of home," I said. "This craziness is too much to take when you arrive from New England in the middle of winter. I feel out of place here, don't you?"

"Not exactly," he said.

"How long have you lived here?"

He flashed me a quick look. "Me or my family?"

I shrugged my shoulders again. "I don't know. Both."

"About a hundred and fifty years," he said seriously.

He grinned again as my mouth dropped open. "You mean you were born here?"

"And my daddy, and his daddy, too. And about three greats before that," he said.

"Your family must have been one of the first families on the Island," I stammered.

"One of the first white families, yes," he said. "But my friend Johnnie over on Maui can trace his family back five hundred years."

I could feel my cheeks flaming with embarrassment. "I feel like such a fool," I said. "You're a Hawaiian, and I said all those rude things."

"Don't worry about it," he said. "Everybody's very open here. We all say what we think. Besides, I don't think you've been here long enough to have an informed opinion. Judging by the color of your skin, I'd say you've only just arrived."

"Last night," I said, feeling more and more stupid. I just wanted to end this conversation and get away.

He looked at me seriously. "That is hardly enough time to get to know anyone or anything."

"I know it's not," I said. "But I guess I'm still depressed about being here and tired after the flight."

"Why would anyone be depressed about coming to Hawaii?" he asked, leaning back against his bicycle and studying me with interest.

I sighed. "It's a long story," I said. "I didn't want to move again. And I didn't want to leave my friends behind."

He nodded his head understandingly. "So you'll be going to high school here?" he asked.

"I guess so."

"You don't sound too enthusiastic," he said. "Make sure you go to Puhoa, not Washington. Puhoa is much more fun. All the kids at Washington think about is studying and more studying. They get better grades, but not by much."

"Puhoa," I said. "I'll remember that."

I noticed a couple of tourists staggering toward us. The woman was wearing a brilliant blue, white, and orange muumuu, decorated in birds and flowers. The man was wearing a matching shirt. They were both loaded down with paper bags and souvenirs. The man was

45

also loaded down with a couple of cameras. He was bald, and the top of his head was red and peeling, matching her face. She saw the boy's bike and came charging over toward him. "Hey, you there—taxi boy!" she shrieked. "Are you free? We want to go back to the Hawaiian Village Hotel." Before he could answer, she dumped her packages into the backseat and climbed in, still shrieking, "You see, Homer, he's free! Get in!"

The boy climbed onto his seat. "You're quite right," he said under his breath to me. "Hawaiians are far too noisy. Give me quiet, dignified mainlanders any day!"

I giggled.

"Come on, get going, we haven't got all day," the woman shouted.

"My name's Jason," he said as he strained at the pedals. "What's yours?"

"Kristy."

"Where do you live?"

"Lanai Apartments. By the canal."

"I know them," he said. "I'll see you, Kristy." He started to bike away, putting all his weight on each pedal to drag the heavy load behind him. His blond hair, slightly too long, blew out behind him as he picked up speed. It was only as he disappeared into the busy traffic that I realized I hadn't even told him my last name. Now he had no way of finding me again, even if he wanted to.

Chapter Six

It took me a few days to recover from jet lag, but my depression never let up. Everybody else on the island seemed to be having a great time. People walked up and down the streets, wearing hardly any clothes and showing off incredible tans. They'd be talking and laughing—really enjoying themselves.

It's OK for them, I thought, scowling behind my new sunglasses. *They can go back where they belong in a couple of weeks. This is just a game for them.*

My family got into the swing of things, too. Dad reported to his new office. He looked so funny going out the door in a dark suit. He said he felt funny, too, and that he'd have to get some light suits made before he died of heatstroke.

Mom spent all her time shopping furiously. There was nothing in the apartment except for the bare essentials. Mom kept discovering more and more things we couldn't live without—a can opener, a potato peeler, a pot holder, and so on. She shopped daily to pick up more necessities.

As for Doug, we had only been in Hawaii for two days before he'd become best buddies with our old Hawaiian doorman and also with Ellen's little brother, Terry. He disappeared down to the Chans' apartment right after breakfast and only showed up again in time for dinner. Then he'd sit at the table giving us the complete life history of every other family in the building.

But I had nothing much to do, except think. I have to confess that some of my thinking was about Jason. He'd seemed so nice and friendly, even though I had insulted him, and I really could have used a friend right then. On the other hand, he was very cute, and I didn't want my emotions torn up again. I'd vowed when I left Massachusetts that I would never fall for another boy, ever. And I could just see my parents' smiles if I brought a new boy home. "So much for Don," they'd say. "You see, we were right. You do get over things quickly at your age."

"Luckily that is not going to happen," I said to myself. "Jason doesn't even know my last name, so there is not much chance of seeing him again."

But I hadn't realized what a small world it was on the Islands. One day I came back from shopping and staggered in with two large bags. I collapsed at the kitchen counter.

"It gets hotter every day here," I panted. "Did Doug finish all that lemonade? I don't think I have the strength to open a new can."

"Kristy," my mother interrupted. "You have a visitor."

"A visitor? Me?" I asked. "Is it Ellen?"

"It's a he," my mother said. "He's out on the *lanai*." She grinned as she said it. "There's a pitcher of lemonade and some glasses out there."

Jason was lying back in the rocking chair, looking very relaxed and content, as if he, not I, lived there. He looked up as I came out and smiled. "Hi," he said simply. He lifted up his glass. "Good lemonade."

I felt my cheeks coloring. "How did you find out where I live?"

He laughed. "One of the first things you'll learn about Hawaii is that there are no secrets on the Islands," he said. "All I had to do was call my friend who lives in these apartments and ask who had just moved in. It took two seconds."

"Heavens," I said. "It's like living with the secret police."

He laughed again. "You'd better believe it," he said. "And it's much worse for me because my family knows everyone. If I take a girl out, my family hears about it the next day. Even if we go somewhere on the other side of the island, you can bet that next morning someone will say, 'Oh, I heard that Jason was over in Kailua yesterday with a new girl. Harry at the gas station said he thought she was the daughter of those new folks over by Koko Head.' "

I laughed, too. "But surely Honolulu is a big place," I said. "Everybody can't know everybody."

"The old-timers all do," Jason said.

"Then I'd better stay away from you if I don't want my comings and goings around the Islands reported daily," I teased.

Jason looked up at me, suddenly serious. I was very conscious of the way his tan complemented his blue eyes. I'd never seen such bright blue eyes before! "If you want to get to know people in a hurry, you *should* stick with me," he said. "I know everyone who's worth knowing here. I know everyone who's not worth knowing, too, so you'll be able to learn the difference."

I laughed uneasily. He hadn't been boasting or joking. Merely stating a fact. "How do you decide?" I asked.

Jason shrugged his shoulders. "Easy," he said. "The fun ones are worth knowing. The boring ones aren't—which brings me to the reason for my visit. One of my friends is giving a beach party this afternoon. A lot of kids from school will be there. I wondered if you'd like to come along. It would be a great chance for you to meet the kids who *are* worth knowing!" He smiled as he said this.

I was beginning to feel more confused. Maybe it was those bright blue eyes that were unnerving me! A beach party did sound like a great way to meet everyone. And if I was with Jason, I had a feeling it would be fun. *Hey, hold on a minute!* a voice inside my head yelled. *Don't start jumping to conclusions. Don't start thinking of this as a date. He probably has a girlfriend, and he's just being kind to a poor, lost newcomer.*

"It sounds like fun," I said hesitantly. "But won't your girlfriend mind if you bring a strange girl along with you?"

He flashed me a teasing grin. "Which girlfriend?" he asked. "I lose count. I change girlfriends about as often as I change my socks. See, when I see a pretty girl, I chase her for a few days. And then when she agrees to go out with me, I lose interest. I'm the type who gets bored easily, I suppose."

This gets better and better, I thought to myself. *This is an invitation for an afternoon with no strings attached. Even if he is interested in me, he'll have lost interest in a few days.*

"So what do you say?" he asked, sitting up and chewing on his sunglasses. "Can you come or not? We'll be over on one of the surfing beaches where the waves are best. The girls usually lie around and sunbathe, unless the boys can sneak up and throw them into the surf, that is. Then around sunset we all have a big barbecue. Someone usually brings a guitar, and we sing in front of the fire—it's great!"

It had sounded great until he mentioned the sunbathing and the being thrown into the water. That brought me back to reality with a jolt. First, I imagined my lily-white body stretched out amid all those dark tans. Then I took the scene a step further and imagined myself having to be pulled, coughing and sputtering, from the surf after they threw me in. An afternoon spent like that would hardly create the best first impression with the kids from a new school.

"Uh, I'm sorry, I just remembered. I promised to look after my little brother while my mom goes out. Thanks a lot, anyway, but I can't come this time."

He got up, uncurling his long body from the low chair. "OK. Well, maybe some other time then," he said easily. "If you want someone to show you around before school starts, just give me a call." He turned to go.

I suddenly realized that my one link with the outside world was walking out of my life, thrown out by me. I sprang after him. "Just a minute, Jason—"

He turned back, and I grinned self-consciously. "I really appreciate your coming by and inviting me today—it's just that today I'm busy, that's all."

"Sure," he said.

"And—Jason—I don't even know your last name, or how to get in touch with you."

"It's Whitmore," he said. "And my number's in the book. Under Whitmore, Jason the third—that's my dad. I'm Whitmore, Jason the fourth. We're an unimaginative family when it comes to names. See you around, Kristy!"

Then he was gone. I stood staring at the doorway, wondering if I should start kicking myself. *I'll probably never see him again now,* I thought, *He has girls around him all the time. He probably won't even remember me by next week, and now I'll never get in with the kids here.*

I remembered how lucky I'd been back in Birchington. By playing soccer I'd met all the most popular girls, and through them I'd met Don. *I bet they don't even play soccer here,* I thought, gloom descending on me again.

"It's OK," I said out loud. "I didn't want to have fun here, anyway."

All the same, I decided that the first thing I had to do was get a tan. I looked like a newly arrived tourist every time I stepped outside. The next thing was to get into shape, then buy myself a sexy bikini. In fact, I could have used a whole new wardrobe. My clothes looked ridiculously East Coast, and at least I wanted to look right when I started school. And to buy all those things, I'd need money. That would mean getting a job. I'd never worked before, except for baby-sitting. I decided that I'd better find a job right away.

I left the apartment and walked down toward Kalakaua Avenue, with no idea where I was going or what I was looking for. I didn't know what sorts of jobs kids could get, but there were certainly lots of stores and restaurants. Something had to be available.

I walked up and down for a while. I didn't have the nerve to go into a store and ask if they wanted extra help, so I just kept on walking. A sign caught my eye: "Part-time help wanted over the holidays and weekends." It was in the window of a Jack-in-the-Box. Still, it was better than nothing. And it *was* only temporary. I walked in and asked for the manager. He took one look at me and frowned. "No, thank you," he said. "I only hire permanent residents."

"But I am a resident," I said.

"Oh, sure," he said, giving me a sarcastic smile. "You look like you stepped off a plane yesterday."

"I did, more or less," I said angrily. "But that doesn't mean that I'm not a resident. You can phone Consolidated Engineering and ask about my father if you like. He works there."

The man's face softened a little. "It's OK. I believe you," he said. "But I have to be careful, you know. These kids come over for two weeks. I train them, then they skip off back to the mainland, and I've wasted all that training for nothing. Ever worked in fast food before?"

"No, but I cooked three hundred hamburgers at summer camp last year," I said. "And I learn quickly."

He nodded. "Well, to tell you the truth, I'm desperate right now," he said. "The place is flooded with tourists. You're hired. Report to me at eight o'clock tomorrow morning, and I'll get someone to train you. I'll have all the papers ready for you to fill out by then."

Feeling excited, I walked out into the sunlight. I wasn't madly excited by the prospect of learning to cook hamburgers and onion rings, but at least I'd found my first job all alone. And soon I would have spending money. When I had a tan and some proper Island clothes, then I could call up Jason again and meet all the kids from Puhoa. I stood at the crosswalk, waiting for the light to change.

Suddenly a motorbike roared past me on the amber light. The driver glanced over his shoulder to check on his surfboard in the back as he swerved past a pedestrian. As I saw his face, I gasped. I clutched the traffic pole, my heart pounding. *It can't be true*, I told myself. *It can't possibly be true!* I watched the bike roar away down the street until it was lost in the traffic. I kept telling myself I hadn't been imagining things. He had the same longish black hair, the same intense, mysterious-looking face, same dark eyes. If the boy on the bike was not Don, then he was alike enough to have been his double!

Chapter Seven

I ran all the way home, arriving back at the apartment out of breath and dripping sweat.

"You should slow down a bit," Ellen said. She was waiting at the elevator as I entered the building. "This isn't Boston, you know. Folks die of heat stroke here."

I leaned against the cool stone of the entrance hall, trying to catch my breath. "I just saw someone I thought I knew," I gasped. "He went by on a motorbike."

Ellen eyed me as if I were not quite right in the head. "And you chased a motorbike?" she asked. "Let me give you a tip—motorbikes go faster than people." She laughed as she said it, and I had to laugh, too.

"No, I didn't chase it," I said. "I'm not quite

that dumb. But I couldn't wait to get home and phone the person I thought I saw to see if it was really him."

The elevator came, and I staggered inside. *Could it really be Don?* I wondered. I wanted it to be him so much. All the way home I'd come up with crazier and crazier reasons why he was here and hadn't called: Don had come over to surprise me; he was secretly practicing surfing to impress me. I flew into the living room. My mother had a pile of college catalogs on the dining table and was busy checking off courses. She looked up as I came in. "Goodness, it must be hot out there today," she said. "We'd all better go for a swim this afternoon."

"Mom," I interrupted. "You know how you said I could phone Don for Christmas. I have a special request. Could I possibly phone him now instead? It's very important."

My mother looked alarmed. "Is something wrong?" she asked.

"No, nothing's wrong," I said. "I just have to ask him something right away. Please, Mom?"

"All right," she said. "We promised to treat you to a call. It's up to you when you make it."

"Great," I said, beaming. I ran to the kitchen where the only phone was. Why couldn't I ever have a phone in my bedroom? At the kitchen door I looked back. "Anyway," I said, "I'll be able to pay for my own phone calls soon. I just got a job at Jack-in-the-Box."

"Hey, that's terrific," my mother said. "Now it seems that everybody's doing something useful with their lives except me."

"Oh, come on, Mom," I said, giving her an encouraging smile. "You keep us all going."

I picked up the phone and dialed. As I heard it ring, I suddenly panicked that it might be the middle of the night over there. But doing some quick figuring, I found out it was only early evening. Don's family would be sitting at the big, scrubbed kitchen table eating dinner.

The phone was answered on the second ring. "Mrs. Partridge, may I please speak to Don," I said, feeling my heart hammering so loudly that I was sure she could hear it over the phone. "This is Kristy."

"Kristy?" she asked, very surprised. "Where are you calling from?"

"From Hawaii."

"Heavens, what a long way. You sound as clear as if you were in the next room. Hold on a second, and I'll get Don." She held the phone away from her mouth and yelled loudly. "Don! Kristy's on the phone! All the way from Hawaii!"

He picked up almost immediately. "Kristy?"

"Don?"

"It's me," he said. "How are you?"

"Oh, I'm fine," I said. "Hot but fine." He laughed. "It's only twelve degrees here. Dad couldn't get the car started this morning. Gosh, I didn't expect to hear from you this soon. I thought your parents were only going to let you phone for Christmas."

"I persuaded Mom to let me call sooner," I said, suddenly feeling like a fool. "I wanted to tell you that I miss you."

"I miss you, too," he said, his voice suddenly low and tender. "You can't imagine the number of times something funny has happened and I've wanted to run back and tell you about it. Then I remember that you're not around to hear."

"I saw a boy today who looks just like you," I said. "For a second I thought it was you."

"Nah," he said. "That can't be true. There can't be two people as good-looking as me in the world."

"He looked exactly like you," I insisted. "You don't have a long-lost twin somewhere, do you?"

"Not unless my mother's been keeping a secret from me all these years!" I heard him yell, "Hey, Ma, did you ever pay a secret visit to Hawaii and not tell anyone?" I could hear laughter at the other end of the phone.

"She said the farthest west she's ever been is Buffalo!" There was more laughter.

"This guy had a surfboard," I went on.

"Then you definitely know that it wasn't a long-lost relative of ours," Don said. "We Partridges get seasick in the bathtub."

We talked a little longer. "I'd better get off the phone," I said. "This must be costing a fortune."

"I'll try to call on Christmas," Don said. "Write

me a long letter telling me all about your mysterious, handsome stranger and who he is, if you ever find out."

"I've already written you two letters," I said. "But I'll let you know about your double. Bye, Don."

"Bye, Kristy." He paused. "Hey, Kristy?"

"Yes."

"I still love you, you know."

"I love you, too, Don."

"That's good. Maybe we'll find a way to be together soon."

"I hope so. I'm going to save money like crazy."

"Me, too. Bye." He made a kissing sound, then I heard the click of the phone as he hung up.

"Bye," I said, hanging up slowly.

Once I knew the boy on the motorbike had nothing to do with Don, I suppose I should have lost interest. But I didn't. I couldn't stop thinking about him. I think that deep inside me a voice was telling me that seeing him was too much of a coincidence, that it must be fate. Right then, I really needed to hold on to something from the past. I wanted to believe that another Don was waiting for me in Hawaii, if only I could meet him.

That, of course, would be a big problem. Honolulu was not the collection of thatched huts I had imagined. When we drove in to see Dad's new office in the business section of town, I saw that it could easily have been Houston or Chicago. Suburbs sprawled out in all directions in Hawaii, too. The odds of meeting the boy were pretty slim. But that didn't stop me from dreaming about him.

So, how do I meet a nameless boy in a city this size? I asked myself, lying on my bed that night. I had my window open because I had already decided that I hated air-conditioning. I could hear the street noises—the drone of passing cars, footsteps tapping on the pavement, and laughter. The scent of the frangipani flowers floated up, too, filling the room with their sweetness. As I lay there, I remembered Jason's words, "I know everybody who's worth knowing. Call me if you want me to show you around!"

I was sure that if the boy lived on the Islands, Jason would know him. I'd call the next day and take Jason up on his offer, if the offer still stood. But I knew I had to be careful not to let him know why I wanted to be shown around. It would hardly flatter his ego to know that I was only with him in the hope of finding another boy!

I didn't have a chance to call him the next morning because I had to report to my new job at eight. A terrifying woman named Zola was in charge of training me. She had enormous beefy arms and a big, booming voice. She had also decided that I must be really dense because she talked to me as if she were talking to a small child. "And this is the money drawer, see? When you punch this key, the drawer opens. Now, let me see you make change. Say the customer gives you two dollars and the purchase came to a dollar twenty-five. Seventy-five cents, right! Very good. You learn real fast!"

By the end of the morning she actually let me take orders for people, although she breathed down my neck the whole time. But everything came in a color-coded box, and I learned which was which pretty quickly. The job wasn't hard, just fast paced. As soon as one order was slapped on a tray, the next person stepped forward, waiting to be served. But problems started if the kitchen didn't have any more hamburgers when a customer had ordered one. Then I had to let the order hang around half finished and remember who was waiting for what! Zola was pleased with me and told the boss I was a good worker. I left work feeling pleased but exhausted at two o'clock. On the way home I thought about the mystery boy. He'd had a surfboard with him, so if I met him, it would probably be on a beach. A great tan was therefore a necessity. I'd never tanned very well. Usually I got freckles and a peeling nose, but no tan. I'd have to look better than that to compete with all the gorgeous local girls. A great idea popped into my head. I'd buy some of that no-sun tanning lotion that came in a bottle! My friend Tina in Houston had tried it one summer. It had been a disaster for her—

she'd put it on at night and dressed right away in her pajamas. The lotion hadn't had a chance to dry, and in the morning her pajamas were brown-and-white striped. So were her legs! We called her zebra all summer! But I was much older and wiser than Tina had been. I'd make sure my legs came out perfectly.

The lady in the pharmacy looked amused when I described what I wanted.

"Why do you need a tan out of a bottle with all that wonderful sun out there?" she asked. "Just go lie on the beach for a few days, and you'll look as good as everyone else."

"But I don't have a few days," I explained. "I want to meet a special boy on the beach, and I've got to look good."

"You young girls," she said, laughing and shaking her head at the same time. "Here, why don't you try this one? I've heard it works pretty well. Not that I ever needed it myself." She gave a big, deep chuckle as she spoke. I looked at her rich, dark skin and laughed, too.

I hurried home and went straight to my room. Doug and Terry Chan were stretched out on the living room floor with rows of little cars, staging a demolition derby. I could still hear them making loud racing car noises as I closed my door. Then Terry yelled, "And he's crashed! The Trans Am is out of the race, folks!"

How lucky little kids are, I thought. *They*

make new friends so easily. They don't have to think about impressing anybody.

I sat on my bed and took out the bottle of Insta-Tan. Looking at my white bedspread, I decided I'd better put it on in the bathroom. It took awhile to cover my body with an even layer. When I was done, I started to examine myself. Just then Doug wanted to come in the bathroom.

"Just a minute!" I yelled back.

"Mom," he yelled. "She won't let me in the bathroom!"

"I said I'll be out in a minute," I called. Doug kept rattling the doorknob until I came out. Then, when he saw me, he burst out laughing. "Hey, you look funny," he said.

"I do not. I've just got a tan, that's all."

"Did you paint yourself with brown paint?"

"No, I did not. It's a tanning product."

"What if it all comes off when you get wet?"

"It won't."

"How do you know?"

"Because it said so on the bottle. Now quit bugging me and go back to your cars."

My mother also looked amused when she saw me. She said she was just shocked to see me looking so different. My dad wasn't so polite. He called me "an instant islander." I thought I looked pretty good. My hair was already beginning to lighten from being in the sun, and the tan made all my clothes look brighter. And I knew I looked healthier.

"At least I don't look like a newly arrived tourist anymore," I said as I went to call Jason.

It took awhile for him to come to the phone, and I could hear a lot of talking in the background. "Yes, it's a girl," someone said. "I don't know what girl, she didn't say. Now will you get on the phone, please?"

"Hi, Jason," I said brightly. "It's Kristy."

"Kristy?" He sounded doubtful. For a horrible moment I thought he'd forgotten who I was. I took a deep breath. "You know—the one you knocked into the flowerpot?" I added. I could hear him give a sigh of relief.

"Oh, Kristy!" he said. "I'm sorry. This girl has been bugging me all week, and her name's Chrissy. I thought you were her. So, what's up?"

"I wanted to take you up on your offer to show me around," I said. "When you've got some free time, of course. I'd really like to meet some of the kids before school starts."

"OK," Jason said easily. "You want to get together tomorrow morning?"

"I'm only free in the afternoons," I said. "I've got a job at Jack-in-the-Box in the mornings."

"Jack-in-the-Box?" He sounded amused. "OK. Afternoon then. What time do you get off work?"

"Two."

"How about if I meet you at two-thirty at your apartment?"

"Great," I said excitedly. "Thanks, Jason."

"Any time."

One more day, I thought excitedly. *Only one more day before I might actually meet Don's double!*

Chapter Eight

The next day I rushed home from work and almost crashed into Ellen again.

"Didn't I tell you to stop running around?" she said, laughing at me. "You're going to kill yourself, girl."

"I've got a boy coming to pick me up in fifteen minutes!" I explained breathlessly as I stepped into the elevator.

"And they say Island girls work fast!" she said. "You've been here less than a week."

I laughed uneasily. "Oh, it's not what you think," I said. "This guy's just being nice. He offered to show me around a bit before I start school."

"You'd better watch yourself. Our Island boys are known to be hot-blooded," she said, her dark eyes flashing at me. The elevator stopped at my floor before I could say any more, and I sprinted down the hall and into my room. What I wore would be very important from then on. After all, who knew when I'd meet Don's double. I flung all my outfits on the bed in disgust. Nothing I had was right. My bathing suit was totally blah. It didn't even show off my new tan. Maybe I should have put off this experiment until I'd earned enough to buy some new clothes. Would Don even notice me if—

Hey, hold on a minute, I reminded myself. *Let's get things straight here. This guy is not Don. Don is your boyfriend back home. You're just curious to meet a guy who looks like Don, but you can't expect him to be Don!*

But however hard I silently lectured myself, part of me was still excited. Part of me wanted to believe that this new boy was somehow connected to Don and to my life in Massachusetts.

Only seconds before Jason was to arrive, I decided to wear my white shorts with a blue halter top. Then I swept my hair into a side ponytail and put on the sort of makeup I saved for evenings. Now that I was tan, I needed brighter, bigger eyes and lips!

Jason was leaning against one of the marble pillars outside my building. He did a double take when he saw me. "Wow," he said. "You sure tan fast!"

I was not going to confess my secret to him, so

I just smiled prettily. I felt good. I could see that Jason liked the way I looked. If I made a good impression on him, who knew what would happen when I met Don's double?

"OK," Jason said as we walked across the sidewalk. "Where do you want to go?"

I thought about the surfboard balanced at the back of that motorbike. "A surfing beach, maybe?" I asked. "A lot of kids go there, don't they?"

He nodded. "Good choice," he said. "Except we don't have any boards."

"Oh, that's fine with me," I said hastily. "I just want to watch anyway. I don't know how to surf."

"I'd better teach you quickly then," he said. "You'll never survive here if you don't know how to surf."

"Give me a chance to settle in first," I said. "I don't think I've ever seen a real big wave before."

He looked amazed, but then he laughed. "Is this your first time near an ocean?" he asked.

"Not exactly," I admitted. "I went to the beach on the East Coast a couple of times, but it was too cold to swim there. I went to Galveston, Texas, too. But there aren't any waves there either."

"We've got plenty of waves here," he said. "Any size you like—up to forty feet over by Makaha."

My mind tried to picture a forty-foot wave and myself standing under it as it crashed down on me. "Uh—do most of the kids go where these forty-foot waves are?" I asked. "Do you surf on the forty-foot waves?"

He shook his head. "Nah, they're just for experts. I've tried the big waves a couple of times, but they scare me. Sometimes we go over to Sunset Beach and the waves are pretty big there. But most of the kids don't want to drive that far every day. Mostly we just go out around Makapuu. I think I'll take you there today."

I looked at him with respect. How many boys would admit to a strange girl that something scared or was too hard for them? Jason was different from anyone I'd ever met. He was so relaxed about things. It was hard to believe that anything would upset him. I followed him down the sidewalk to where a bright yellow motorbike was parked.

"OK. Climb on," he instructed.

"Does everyone ride motorbikes here?" I asked before I'd really thought about it.

He looked puzzled. "Everyone?" he asked. "I ride one because I like the feel of the wind on my face."

He swung himself onto the bike, and I noticed he wasn't wearing shoes. Didn't anybody wear shoes, either? I'd have to learn to toughen my feet! Cautiously I climbed onto the bike behind him, suddenly very conscious of his closeness. He turned back to me. "Hold on tight," he said.

"There are some pretty sharp bends up ahead, and I don't want to lose you over a cliff."

I wrapped my arms around his waist, glad that he couldn't see my pink, embarrassed face. He gunned the engine, and we shot forward. We sped along the road by the canal and then through a shady park. Then we passed through a beautiful residential area. Gardens of huge bushes and blossoming vines and tall, flowering trees spilled over walls into the roadway. I must confess that I couldn't see them too clearly. I was barely conscious of the flashes of color and the sweet scents. Mostly I was concentrating on not falling off the bike when we went around sharp bends! I had never ridden on a motorbike before, and the sensation of speed was terrifying. The pavement flashed by us, and the wind snatched at our clothes. Every time we went around a corner the bike seemed to lean at an impossible angle. I wondered if Jason could feel my arms trembling and what he would think.

By the time we started the climb up Diamond Head, I had relaxed enough to enjoy the feel of the sweet, salty wind on my face. We passed more and newer suburbs, then I saw a second volcano ahead of us. The road swung over its tail, and Jason pulled off into a parking lot and stopped.

"That's Hanauma Bay," he said, pointing down. A circle of clear blue water, fringed with white sand, lay below us. Waves were breaking outside the reef, but inside, the water was totally still.

"It's beautiful," I said.

"It's where people go to snorkel and feed the fish," Jason said. "You can stand there with bread in your hand and they all swim up to you."

That seemed like a more sensible occupation than standing under forty-foot waves. "Terrific," I said.

I was about to suggest that we skip the surfing beach and go there instead when Jason said, "Of course, the place is crawling with tourists. The natives never go there anymore. Let's go, OK?"

"Sure," I said, turning to walk back to the bike.

After a wild ride along the shore, we finally turned off the main road and into a parking lot overlooking a small, sandy beach. Down below I could see neat lines of surf coming in and heads bobbing out beyond it, waiting for the next wave.

Jason stopped the bike and looked down. "Oh, great, Tom and Alex are here," he said. "And no tourists. Let's go down."

We parked under a couple of palm trees beside two more new motorbikes and several old, rusty clunkers. When Jason turned the engine off, I could hear the crash and roar of the waves as they broke, followed by a hiss as they rushed onto the beach. The waves didn't look so small and harmless at shore level. Several kids were bodysurfing. Their heads bobbed in the great foaming mass of water before they were flung up onto the sand. Jason walked ahead of me toward a bunch of towels where several bikini-clad girls were lying stretched out on their stomachs.

As we approached them, one of the girls got up and started to rub more suntan oil on her arm. She looked up, and her face broke into a delighted smile. "Well, look who's here, everybody," she announced. "I haven't seen you since we got out of school."

The other girls turned over and sat up, all of them smiling at Jason. "We thought you'd given us up," one of the girls said.

"Or given up surfing."

They teased one another the way that old friends do, and I stood there, invisible to them, feeling shy. Then one of them noticed me and stared at me with obvious interest. "Are you going to introduce your friend?" she asked in a lilting, musical voice. "Is she the one who's been keeping you away from us?"

Jason looked back at me with amusement. "Her?" he asked. "No—this is Kristy. She's a *malihini.*"

"Really?" The girls looked even more interested and amused. I felt like a fish in an aquarium, doubly embarrassed because I didn't know what a *malihini* was.

"And where did you find her?" a tall, dark girl

asked, tossing her heavy black hair over her shoulders.

"I found her in a flowerpot," Jason said, squatting down beside them and looking up at me. He gave me a wink.

"Oh, come on now," the dark girl said.

Jason turned his innocent, blue eyes in my direction. "It's true. Right, Kristy?" he asked.

"Only after you knocked me into the flowerpot in the first place," I answered, glad to have a chance to join the conversation.

Jason laughed. "I was driving Steve's pedicab for him. Those things are tough to steer, you know. I had to swerve, and when I did I knocked her backward into a tub of flowers."

The dark girl sighed. "Leave it to you, Jason, to think of a new way to pick up girls," she said. She turned to me and smiled. "Where are you staying?"

"Oh, we're not staying—I mean, we're going to be living here," I said. Everyone started laughing as if I'd said something funny. I looked at Jason, and he grinned. "Over here, staying and living mean the same thing. What Luana wanted to say was—what is your address?"

"Oh," I said, embarrassed again. "The Lanai Apartments, by the canal. We're living there until our furniture arrives. I'm sorry I didn't understand you. I had no idea that I'd have a language problem over here."

A little blond with bouncy curls sat up beside

Launa. "Oh, wait till they all start talking pidgin," she said. "When we first moved here, I couldn't understand a word."

"What's pidgin?" I asked suspiciously, wondering if she was pulling my leg.

"It's what the uneducated islanders speak," she said. "And these guys, too, when they don't want tourists to understand them. Like—when dis *aikane kama'aini* give you de eyeball."

"Hey, dass no big ting, brah," Jason interrupted, and they all laughed, leaving me feeling confused and left out. Clearly it was not going to be easy to get in with a new group.

"Are you going to go to our school?" the blond asked me.

"I hope so," I said.

"Of course she's coming to our school," Jason interrupted. "Where else would she go?" One of the guys yelled to Jason from out beyond the breakers. He grabbed a spare board and ran toward the water.

"You want to try?" he called back to me.

"Not today, thanks," I said. "You go ahead."

He didn't need any more persuading and charged into the waves. That left me alone with the girls. Luana scooted over beside me, handing me her bottle of oil. "Better put it on before you burn," she said. "Jason didn't introduce us. I'm Luana, and this is Kelly and Julie and Sharon and Tui."

The other girls gave me a nod and a smile and went back to sunbathing.

Luana leaned on her elbows beside me. "So, how long have you been going with Jason?" she asked, watching me coolly.

I laughed uneasily. "Oh, it's not like that," I said. "We just started talking after the whole thing with the flowerpot. He offered to show me around over the vacation. I think he felt sorry for me because I didn't want to be here."

A smile spread across Luana's face. "No way. Jason Whitmore would never spend time with a girl because he felt sorry for her. If he shows up more than once, he's interested in you. Believe me."

"Oh, I don't think so," I said, feeling confused. "He's just a nice person, and he understands that it's not easy to move in the middle of a school year."

"Sure," Luana said. "Well, we'll see—" she said, stopping midsentence and staring at me. "Are you looking for somebody special?" she asked. "Or are you just giving all the boys the once-over?"

"No, why?" I asked, embarrassed by her strange question.

"Because you keep looking around. Every time a boy comes in on a wave, you take a little peek at him," she said, grinning. Until she mentioned it, I hadn't realized that I'd been doing that. But she was right. I had been looking at every boy to see if he was the boy who looked like Don.

Luana got to her feet. "I feel like a swim. It's too hot here in the sun," she said. "You want to come?"

I stared out at that churning, crashing water. "I—uh—don't think so, thanks," I said.

"Oh, come on," she insisted. "You'll get to meet the boys close up," she added teasingly.

"Those waves look kind of big," I admitted.

"I'm just going to splash around at the edge," she said. "I don't want to get sand in my hair. Come on."

Even I didn't mind splashing around by the shore. I stood up and peeled off my shorts and top, horribly conscious of my conservative bathing suit.

"I haven't had time to get myself a bikini yet," I explained.

"But at least you've got a nice tan already," Luana said. I couldn't tell whether she suspected it was fake or not. Her comment reminded me of what my brother had said. What if the tan really did come off in saltwater? I'd look like a fool in front of everyone. I almost sat down again, but I was feeling pretty hot by then, and the water did look cool and inviting. And there were lots of boys out there.

The first waves felt heavenly against my burning feet and sandy legs. The water was cool but not cold. Nervously looking down at my legs, I saw that they were as perfectly tan as before. I walked out a little farther, feeling the slap and pull of the waves as they rushed in. Luana waited for a smooth patch of water, then swam away. She was sleek as a dolphin, her brown arms cutting through the water with almost no splash. I knelt down cautiously, getting up again as the next wave came rushing in. At the next smooth patch, I tried swimming, too, and found that it was very easy to float. Now, if only I knew something other than the dog paddle.

Some of the other girls had come to join us. They were all around me, diving through waves and swimming out to the boys. I didn't want them to see my clumsy attempt at swimming, so I concentrated on watching the surfers. I saw Jason ride in smoothly, turning his board around with ease, keeping with the waves as long as possible. A couple of other boys came in, too, shaking water from their dark, curly heads. I felt like such a wimp standing there, so I turned my back to the ocean, looking up to the tall cliffs beyond. Some sea gulls overhead caught my eye, and I watched them circling lazily. Then suddenly—wham! The wave was upon me before I heard it. The first thing I felt was its powerful force on the back of the neck. I felt myself being flung forward, tumbling over and over. Sand and water were everywhere. I fought to stand up and couldn't. Water was in my mouth, stinging my eyes. I suppose it only took a couple of seconds, but it felt like forever before the wave passed me and I could put my feet on the sandy bottom again. I stood up, coughing, spluttering, and feeling like a fool. I looked around to see if any of the kids had seen my stupid performance. Thankfully, nobody was near me. All that was there was a gray fin, cutting through the water, coming closer and closer. I froze, paralyzed with fear. Memories of the old *Jaws* movies came rushing into my mind. Finally I forced my mouth open. "Shark!" I screamed. "Shark! Help!"

The effect was instantaneous. Just like in the movies, people started running from the ocean screaming. "Where? Where's the shark?" kids were yelling.

Kelly's head broke the surface nearby. "Hey, did anybody see my board?" she yelled. "I lost it on that last big wave. It's gray—" She reached out and grabbed the fin. "Oh, here it is," she said. "Alex would kill me if I lost it. Hey, what's everybody doing?" She looked from one worried face to the next.

When she picked up the surfboard, I could see that it didn't look like a shark at all. Jason arrived, shaking the water from his hair. "What's happening?" he asked.

"Somebody was screaming about a shark," one of the girls said.

"Where's a shark?" Jason asked. "Sharks

don't come in here. I've never heard of anyone seeing a shark here."

"I'm sorry," I said. "It was me—I saw the fin on Kelly's surfboard floating toward me, and I thought it was a shark."

Everybody laughed loudly, but I didn't think it was funny.

Chapter Nine

That evening I sat alone in my room, playing tapes and thinking about the day. We hadn't stayed at the beach very long after the shark incident.

The kids can't have thought too much of me, I told myself, brushing savagely at the salty, sandy tangles in my hair. *It really wasn't the greatest first impression. Maybe I shouldn't go to their school after all. Maybe I belong with the brains at the other high school.* The trouble was that they'd all seemed like nice people—especially Jason. I was really confused about him. I'd felt comfortable with him from the very start. I liked him, and I'd been sure he was just being friendly until Luana said that he must be interested in me. After that I'd felt self-conscious around him. I looked for signs that he was treating me the way a boy treats a girl when he's interested. I didn't see any. He talked to me as if I were a kid sister.

So Luana was totally wrong, I'd figured while we were riding home on the bike. *Maybe she has a crush on Jason herself and she's jealous of me.* I felt relieved that Jason wasn't secretly falling in love with me. After all, even if I did enjoy his company, I was just using him to meet another guy.

Any doubts about Jason were swept away when we got home. He deposited me outside my building, and I dismounted stiffly.

"Well, thanks again," I said hesitantly. "I'm glad I met some of your friends, and I'm sorry about the shark stuff."

He smiled. I noticed that the corners of his eyes crinkled up when he smiled and I thought it was cute. "Forget about it," he said. "Anyone who's never seen an ocean before could make the same mistake. I'll bet I'd get a snowman mixed up with Bigfoot if I was ever up north! You want to come to the beach with me again, or have you lost your nerve?"

I thought about Don's double. I couldn't give up the hunt so easily. "I'd like that a lot," I said. "And I guess I'd better learn to surf sometime. I don't want everyone here to think I'm chicken."

"That's my girl," Jason said, giving me a

friendly pat on the arm. "We'll go out again real soon."

"Thanks for everything, Jason," I said.

He flashed me a broad grin. "Don't worry, you're doing me a favor, too," he said. "Remember that girl I told you about, the one who keeps calling? Well, now my friends will spread the word that I've been bringing a new girl to all the beaches with me, and maybe she'll cool off!" He laughed and waved casually as he walked back to his bike and swung himself onto the seat. "See you, Kristy," he said, starting the engine with a roar. "I'll call you, OK?"

Then he was gone. *So there you are, Luana*, I thought, looking in the mirror as I got the last tangles out of my hair. *He's only using me to keep another girl away. Nothing to worry about at all.*

One other thing I decided that evening was that I most definitely had to learn to swim. I hated the thought of being looked at as a wimpy mainlander. I'd finally found out that *malihini* meant stranger. I didn't want to be one for long. All my life I'd been pretty athletic. I'd taken gymnastics and worked out on a balance beam, so I figured I could learn to ride a surfboard, too.

The next morning I came right out with it at breakfast. "Mom, I think I need swimming lessons," I said as I poured my bowl of cereal. "I'm never going to fit in here if I can't swim well."

"I agree," my mother said, looking up from the

stove where she was breaking eggs into the frying pan. "Dad and I were saying last night that Doug ought to have lessons right away. He keeps wanting to go down to the beach with Terry, and I don't think he swims well enough to be trusted alone yet. I'll find out about swim schools this morning, and maybe we can even get a lesson for you both this afternoon."

She did, and that afternoon after work we all took a taxi to a public pool over in Honolulu. The pool was full of small, brown bodies. Mom gave our names to a girl with a clipboard, and we stood around while kids were gathered into groups.

"You mean we don't get a private lesson?" I whispered to her.

She shrugged helplessly. "You should have seen the cost of private lessons," she whispered back. "It's this or nothing."

"Douglas Johnson, Kristy Johnson," the girl called. Doug started to walk toward the pool. I grabbed my mother's arm. "I am positively not going to join this class," I said. Apart from Doug the oldest kid in the class was around four. About ten little kids had already jumped into the water. They dove under water and swam around like little fish. I was not going to have them giggling at me when I tried to put my face in the water.

"You can stay," I said. "I'm going home."

"Suit yourself," my mother said evenly. "It's up to you if you want to learn to swim."

"I'll teach myself, thank you," I said and left. I caught a bus back to Waikiki and walked through the hotel to the beach. "OK. So I'll teach myself to swim," I said calmly. One section of beach was especially calm. The waves were blocked by a big wall running all around it. I walked into the warm, calm water and started to swim. It wasn't hard at all.

"Great," I said to myself. "Now put your face in the water." That part was a little trickier. I shut my eyes tightly and kicked forward while the water went up my nose. I put my feet down and came up spluttering.

"You look funny," a voice said beside me. A little girl was watching me. "Don't you know how to swim?" she asked curiously.

"Yes, of course I do," I said. "I was just trying something out."

"It's easy," she said. "You have to open your eyes, or you can't see where you are going. Then you just do a rocket. Watch me!"

She stretched out her arms and propelled herself along like a streamlined torpedo. It did look easy when she did it.

"Very good," I said.

"I can do lots of things," she went on, having decided that she had an admiring audience. "Watch me. I can run along the wall."

Before I could say anything, she climbed up

onto the slippery stones and started to run. "Hey, I don't think you'd better do that!" I yelled after her. "Come back!"

As I was shouting, she stumbled and pitched forward into the water. I waited, holding my breath, for her to come up again. She didn't. She was only a few yards away from me. Surely even I could swim that far under water? I took a deep breath and plunged forward. The water stung at my eyes, but not so much as the chlorine in swimming pools had. And I could see. The water was clear, and I could pick out the dark line of the seaweed-covered wall ahead. A school of little white fish flicked aside as I plunged toward them. I kicked my feet like crazy and thrashed with my arms. I could see a little white body turning over in the water. I grabbed her, and we both shot to the surface, gasping for air.

I think I half expected to see a crowd gathered, all cheering my brave deed. At the very least I expected the little girl to cry and tell her mommy how I had saved her. Instead, an angry little face stared at me. "What did you do that for?" she asked. "You pulled my hair."

"I saved you from drowning," I said angrily.

"I wasn't drowning," she said angrily. "I was seeing how long I could hold my breath."

"Oh," I said, not knowing whether to believe her or not. "Well, don't run along that wall again or next time you *will* drown."

In spite of not being a hero, I still went home

pretty happy. I could swim if I had to. I could even swim underwater. The water did not do terrible things to my eyes. It wouldn't even get up my nose if I breathed out. I might not do an elegant crawl stroke like Luana had done, but I could still learn to surf!

The next two days before Christmas were pretty busy. And Waikiki was swarming with tourists. Zola at Jack-in-the-Box begged me to work extralong shifts. I didn't see or hear anything from Jason, and I felt funny calling him. He'd told me that he got tired of girls very quickly. Maybe he'd already lost interest in me, and I'd never get to go to the surfing beaches with him again. That was the kind of depressing thought that occupied my head. It went along well with my mood, which was pretty down.

I suppose the real problem was Christmas. Even though we'd moved around a lot, I had never spent Christmas away from all my relatives before. Usually Grandma Johnson would come up from Florida, or we'd go to visit Mom's parents in Pennsylvania. This year we'd have nobody. And even worse, it wouldn't even feel like Christmas. How could anyone get into the holiday spirit when there were palm trees outside and the temperature was eighty degrees? Even Mom was halfhearted about baking her usual goodies. "Isn't it too hot for stollen?" she asked. "And surely nobody wants mince pies in this weather?" No one seemed to, but me. I wanted everything to be the same. Holidays should be a series of traditions, I'd always thought, from the order in which we unwrapped our presents to what we ate for dinner. It seemed that nobody in my family cared about traditions except me. They didn't care if Christmas dinner was cold turkey eaten on the beach, followed by ice cream. They didn't even care if we had a tree or not.

And the tree was the worst of all. For the first time in my life we didn't have a live Christmas tree. My parents had gone out and bought a terrible plastic one. I hated it so much that I couldn't even look at it, much less help decorate it.

"It doesn't smell right or anything," I told them. "It's phony, like everything else here. It belongs with the tinsel hula skirts."

"Fine. Don't help if you don't want to," my brother said. "I'll get to put the angel on the top this year!"

I went out and left them to their decorating. Just as I got off the elevator, I saw Jason coming in through the big, glass doors.

"Hey, *Mele Kalikimaka!*" he called.

"What's that supposed to mean?" I shot back. "You know I don't speak the language."

"That's Merry Christmas in Hawaiian!" he said.

"Doesn't feel very merry to me," I muttered.

"How come?" He looked surprised.

I sighed. "Oh, I guess I'm just feeling gloomy again," I said, attempting to smile. "They're all upstairs decorating a plastic tree. It just doesn't seem right to me. I can remember how good the real trees smelled when we went out to the forest. We'd take a long time choosing one, then brush the snow off the branches and carry it home."

"Holidays always make people homesick," he said. "We'd better do something to take your mind off things. I came by because my friends and I are having a big Christmas beach party over on the north shore, and I wondered if you'd like to come?"

"Great," I said. "Can you hold on a minute, and I'll get my swimsuit? And I'd better put on long pants, for the motorbike."

"Oh, I've got the car today," he said. "But go get your suit. I've also got a couple of boards. You can try surfing!"

Minutes later we were speeding out through pineapple fields in the little red sports car that belonged to Jason's brother. After the pineapple fields came sugarcane and then wild, windy country dotted with little wooden shacks. We met up with the ocean again near a long, straight beach. Enormous waves were rolling in, surfers riding high on the crests. I looked at them in horror.

"We're not going there, are we?" I asked.

Jason laughed. "Relax. That beach is for

experts. You'll be fine where we're going." And soon we pulled up at another long, sandy beach where a big group of kids was already sitting round a fire. Luana and some of the other girls were there, and they greeted me like an old friend.

"So, are you going to try surfing today?" Luana asked me.

"I don't know," I said, looking doubtfully at the waves. "They look kind of big to me!"

"Oh, come on, Kristy," Jason said. "You promised you were going to learn. I've even brought you a nice little beginner board."

I studied the waves even harder. They didn't look like the nice, gentle waves at Waikiki. Maybe I'd wait and start my lessons there. Another carload of kids arrived. We would hear the loud music as their car pulled up. Five of them got out, all carrying boards, and ran down toward the ocean.

"Man, this beach is too tame today," one of the boys called.

"Well, I'm not doing the pipeline today," a second boy yelled back. "I'm not breaking my neck."

I looked over at them and almost jumped. The speaker was Don's double. He was carrying a long blue board and walking into the surf. Even seen close up he looked exactly like Don. I could hear his voice echoing out across the water, and it was deep just like Don's. I watched him disappearing out into the waves. They were breaking all around him when he turned and looked back. His dark, smoldering eyes stared past me to the kids up the beach. "Are you guys coming or not?" he called.

"Be right with you, Darren," someone called back.

That made me jump even more. Darren. His name was Darren. Wasn't that too close to Don to be a coincidence? I got to my feet. "I've decided," I said, sounding more brave than I really felt, "I *am* going to learn to surf today."

Jason jumped up beside me. "Good girl," he said. "Here, grab the board."

We waded out through the waves. The water was not deep there, but the waves were strong, and they threatened to knock me over. At last we were out about waist deep, holding on to our boards. Out of a corner of my eye, I watched Darren and his buddies come rushing past us on a wave. *If only I could do that,* I thought. Maybe then he'd notice me. Maybe I'd even get a chance to talk to him.

Jason told me to straddle the board, wait for the wave, and start paddling. Then he showed me how to lie across it and stand up. He made it seem very easy. It wasn't. To begin with, by the time I got paddling fast enough, the wave had passed me by. Then, when I caught a wave by accident, and felt the speed surge me forward, I was much too chicken to let go of my board. I lay there, holding on for dear life, as we rushed toward the shore.

"Great," Jason said encouragingly. "You're getting the idea really fast. Now next time all you have to do is kneel on the board and then gradually get to your feet."

"Oh, sure," I said, laughing. "That's all, huh?"

He laughed, too. "It's not that hard, really," he said. "I'll tell you what. You kneel on the board and I'll hold it and get you started at the right moment."

We tried it. I squatted on the board, and a wave came rushing toward us. Jason gave me a mighty shove, and suddenly I was hurtling toward the shore. I could feel the speed. The wind was in my face. Spray was all around me.

"Now stand up," Jason was yelling. Very gradually I got to my feet. I felt terrific. I was actually standing on a surfboard. *Let him look up and notice me right now*, I prayed. *Let everyone notice me, but especially Darren.* Without moving my balance at all, I tried to look around to see where he was. Then I saw him standing with a group of kids at the water's edge. They were just about to walk out for another run. None of them even noticed me hurtling toward them.

Suddenly I realized that I didn't know how to stop.

"Jason," I yelled behind me. "How do you stop this thing?"

I was getting closer and closer, and the wave

93

was not losing speed at all. I tried to yell, but they didn't hear me. At the last moment they looked up and saw me flying toward them. Instantly they flung themselves left and right as my board crashed through the middle of them and plowed straight into Darren. I was flung off the board and slapped into the shallow water so forcefully that the wind was knocked out of me.

As I went under, I wondered for a fleeting second if Darren would rescue me. Would our eyes meet as he dragged me to the surface? I staggered to my feet, and my eyes did meet his. Those dark, flashing eyes were gazing right at me. He opened his mouth to speak to me.

"Of all the stupid, crazy things," he said in Don's smooth, deep voice. "What did you think you were doing? You might have hurt somebody!"

Before I could think of anything to say, a voice spoke up behind me. "It was her first time on a board, OK?" Jason said, sliding to a halt beside me. "She can't control it yet. I thought she did pretty well."

The dark eyes looked at me coldly. "I suggest that she go back to the kiddy beach until she learns how to use that thing," Darren said. "She's dangerous to have around." He turned and paddled out after his friends.

"Hey, don't listen to him," Jason said, seeing my bleak face. "Just because some nobody insults you—forget it. I think you were fantastic. Who cares what that bozo thinks?"

I couldn't tell him that I did care. I cared very much because I had just wrecked my one chance to meet the only boy I cared about.

Chapter Ten

The next few days of Christmas and after were pretty bad. In fact, I can honestly say that they were the low point of my life. Christmas Day came and went. I really couldn't get excited about it, even though it was the first year when I could buy my family presents with my own money. I got some great gifts, too, especially the blue-and-yellow bikini and matching cover-up from my mother. I tried to look pleased because I could tell from her face that she had gone to a lot of trouble to choose it. But inside I told myself that I wouldn't ever need it. I wouldn't be going to the beach again. I wouldn't be going anywhere now that I had blown my chance with Darren.

Every time I thought of that day at the beach, I squirmed with embarrassment. I could remember Darren's dark eyes, so like Don's, flashing at me angrily. Of course, he'd had every right to be angry. I could have seriously hurt him, flying out of control the way I did. But after that whole fiasco he'd never want to get to know me better, even if we *did* meet again. I felt that fate had offered me a wonderful promise and I had failed. Even a phone call from the real Don back in Birchington didn't cheer me up. He sounded so cheerful, and I could hear laughter and music in the background as he spoke.

"I got that job with my uncle," he said excitedly, "And I've bought a really big piggy bank. So don't be surprised if I turn up on your doorstep this summer. And you'd better not have too many other boys hanging around when I come!"

Maybe it's a good thing I didn't meet Darren, I thought afterward. That would be the the most embarrassing thing in the world—having Don and Darren standing there, staring at each other, maybe even fighting over me!

"Don't worry, Don," I'd told him. "There won't be any boys hanging around. I'm going to devote my life to good deeds from now on." He had laughed. He didn't think I was serious, but I was. From then on, I would definitely stay away from boys.

Not that that was a very hard thing to do. Jason didn't show up again, and I caught a glimpse of him only once. He flashed by in the red sports car with another girl beside him. I felt a stab of jealousy as I watched them disappear. At least Jason could cheer me up. He'd been a patient tour guide, and he'd defended me when Darren had yelled. But obviously I was not a fun person to have around. In fact, I was an embarrassment. I yelled about sharks and crashed into people on surfboards.

I was thinking all this over as I wandered down the hall one afternoon. I'd been going on long walks after work and had discovered some fascinating things. There was Duke's Alley, a place filled with stalls where you could bargain for everything. And the zoo where you could get in for free and climb a platform and look the giraffes in the eye. That afternoon I'd planned to walk in the opposite direction from them, down toward the big shopping center where they had some good sales going on. But before I reached the elevator, Ellen came out of her door.

"Hey, Kristy, wait up," she yelled, running barefoot down the hall toward me. "I've got a whole afternoon off, and I'm heading for the beach. Want to come along?"

"Not today," I said.

"Oh, where were you going?" she asked, her face falling.

"To Ala Moana Center," I said.

"Oh, come on. It's much too nice a day to go shopping," she said. "And I hate going to the beach by myself. I haven't even seen you in that new bikini you got for Christmas."

Her big, dark eyes pleaded with me. I sighed. "Oh, all right. I'll go get changed."

Ten minutes later we were lying on large, inflatable plastic mattresses on the still, blue water, rocking gently as the small waves ran beneath us.

"This is the life," Ellen said. "Now aren't you glad you left all that cold snow behind?"

"Not really," I said. "I still miss my friends."

"A special friend?" Ellen asked, looking at me through her dark cascade of hair.

"Yes," I admitted.

She laughed. "I wondered why you were such an old grouch," she said. "But what happened to the Hawaiian boy who was chasing you or who you were chasing? I forget which."

"It's a long story," I said, watching my hand float below me in the water and brush against a delicate ribbon of seaweed.

"We've got all afternoon," Ellen said. "You want to tell me about it?"

Suddenly I wanted to tell somebody. I spilled out everything—about Don and Jason and Darren. Every painful detail. "So, I guess I'm going to go through another two years with no friends," I said and sighed. When I had finished, I waited for Ellen to sympathize with me. Instead she sat up on her air mattress and frowned at me.

"You know what your trouble is, don't you?" she said fiercely. "You're too wrapped up in your-

99

self. So you had to leave your boyfriend behind. That's sad, but you can't just spend the rest of your life moping about it. And you can't really expect to be handed a perfect new boyfriend the moment you step off the plane, just because he happens to look like your boyfriend back home! And now you're determined to feel sorry for yourself and have a bad time here. If you think that way, you *will* have a bad time. You'll hate it here, and that's the stupidest thing you could do. I like the way you say you don't have any friends. Well, I thought I was your friend. If I didn't, I wouldn't be talking to you like this."

As she talked, I got angrier and angrier. When she finished, I slid off my mattress into the water with a splash. "If you were my friend, you wouldn't talk to me like that," I said coldly. "You don't understand. You don't know what it's like to keep on moving around."

"No, I don't," Ellen said. "But I know I wouldn't keep sulking about it, going around with my chin down to my knees."

"I do not," I said.

"Go look at yourself in the mirror sometime," she snapped.

"I'm going home," I said, dragging the mattress out of the water. "I'll leave your mattress up with the towels."

Ellen shrugged her shoulders. "Good idea," she said. "Shut yourself in your room again, just like you've been doing since you got here."

"Did anyone ever tell you you're a pain?" I yelled back at her.

A grin flashed across her face. "Frequently," she said. "But I've never let that stop me."

I slid into my thongs and stomped off up the beach. All the way home my head was boiling with angry thoughts. Who did she think she was, talking to me like that? I hardly knew the girl. I didn't even want her as a friend. I didn't want any of them—not Luana, not Darren who had yelled at me, and not even Jason who had a new girl in his car. None of them cared about me.

I flung the door open and stomped into the apartment. I heard a hasty rustling of papers and feet running. My immediate thought was that Doug had been in my room, reading my diary or something. I rushed toward the noise and surprised not Doug, but my mother. She was standing in the bathroom clutching a big sheaf of papers, with tears running down her cheeks.

"Oh, Kristy," she stammered, trying to brush them away with the back of her hand. "I didn't expect—I thought you'd gone out—"

"What's the matter, Mom," I asked. "What's wrong?"

"Nothing," she said, brushing away the last tear. "It's nothing. I'm just being silly, that's all."

"Is there some kind of trouble?" I asked. "You can tell me."

She shook her head. "It's really nothing, Kristy. I'm being stupid really. It's just that the mail arrived, and they said my college courses are all full."

I stood and stared at her just like Ellen had stared at me. I had expected something really terrible. I'd thought she'd been told she had an incurable disease or that Dad was moving out or that Grandma had died. Something as bad as that. Not just a college course being full! I almost laughed. I did smile a little and she saw it.

"I know you think that's no big thing," she said sadly.

"There'll be plenty of time to sign up for more courses, Mom," I said.

She gave a big sigh. "I don't think you understand," she said. "I don't think anybody does. My courses are all I have. Your father has his work, and you and Doug make friends in school. I'd never meet anybody if I didn't go to all these classes. It's so lonely sometimes. . . ."

I stared at her as if I were seeing a new person. This wasn't my mother who was always cheerful when we came home from school. Instead I saw a lonely woman who kept herself busy with cooking and painting and aerobics and psychology so that she could shut out the loneliness in her life. And I also saw that Ellen had been right. I had been too wrapped up in myself. I'd thought I was the only one who suffered when we moved. I'd been too busy feeling sorry for myself to notice anyone else.

I went forward and put my arms around her. "I do understand, Mom," I said. "You wanted to take those courses a lot and getting the letter saying they were full was the last straw, right? Maybe it's going to take us both a little while to land on our feet here. I guess we'd better stick together. Let's go out and look over the after-Christmas sales."

She nodded, her face shining with tears like a little girl's. "Oh, Kristy," she said. "I'll go wash my face and put on some makeup."

Chapter Eleven

That evening Ellen came by to see me. "Listen, Kristy," she said, standing in the doorway and wiggling her toes in embarrassment, "I'm sorry about this afternoon. I have a big mouth. All my family says so. I had no right to speak to you like that."

"But what you said was true," I admitted. "I realized afterward that you were right. I'd been thinking of myself so much that I didn't notice anyone else."

"But I had no right to yell at you like that," Ellen said. "I was treating you like family. I forgot you aren't Island people. You probably don't say what's on your mind the way we do. You must think I'm the rudest person."

I smiled. "I'm getting used to you, Ellen," I

said. "And I'd like you to go on treating me like family. It makes me feel like I belong."

"Great," she said, beaming at me. "You want to come down to our place for dinner? My mother makes the best spareribs."

After that life got pretty busy as Doug and I prepared for school.

"I wish I was going to school with you," I told Ellen. "It'll be terrible going through that door on the first day all by myself."

Ellen wrinkled her nose. "You wouldn't want my school," she said. "For one thing we have to wear a uniform that makes us look like orphans from a hundred years ago! Black and white sailor suits. *And* it's all girls. *And*, worst of all, they give you tons of homework."

"So why do you go there?" I asked. "Everybody says that Puhoa is more fun."

Ellen lifted her heavy black hair from her face. "You've met my father," she said. "He's very hot on education. His mother went to my school. His sisters all went there. Now I've got to suffer through it. I guess one of the good things about moving around like you do is that you won't ever be forced to follow in your family's footsteps."

"I don't know," I said. "Right now I'd give anything not to have to start at another strange school."

"Oh, you'll be fine," Ellen said. "The kids are very friendly here."

But on the first morning, it didn't seem that way at all. I walked up the front steps of the old-fashioned, square building along with hundreds of other kids, and I might as well have been invisible. I sat through four invisible classes. I ate an invisible lunch in the shade of a huge old tree out behind the building. I had come to school with a lot of good intentions. I'd promised myself and Ellen that I'd make an effort to like it here. But I could hardly get along with people if nobody ever spoke to me.

That first day was like being on another planet. The kids swept through the halls, tanned bodies in flowered shirts and cutoffs, talking and laughing in a language I couldn't always understand. They spoke a mixture of English and pidgin, with a few Hawaiian words thrown in. When our papers were collected in one class, the boy ahead of me asked if I was *pau* and I said, "No, I'm Kristy." Everyone started giggling. Then the teacher explained that *pau* meant finished. I left the room with a red face, feeling their giggles following me down the hall.

As I left that class, I saw Jason, the first familiar face all day.

"Hey, Kristy, how are you doing?" he called, grabbing my arm as I hurried to find the science wing.

"Surviving, barely," I said. "I feel like I'm drowning in a sea of strange people."

He smiled. "I guess we're a noisy bunch, right?"

"It's not so much the noise, it's the numbers," I said. "I've just come from a school of three hundred and fifty. Here there are that many kids in line for the bathroom."

"It'll get better," he said. "Meet us for lunch tomorrow—we're out by the football field."

"Jason, hurry up," a voice yelled somewhere ahead of us in the crowd. "You're going to make me late!" The crowd parted, and I saw a little blond girl in a bright red miniskirt waving frantically at him.

Jason looked at me and sighed. "Got to run," he said. "See you around, Kristy."

Then he left. My only contact with the kids at school—and he was chasing after yet another girl. I stood there in the hall, overcome with panic. I was never going to fit in there, no matter how hard I tried. How could I possibly make friends if nobody even slowed down enough to notice me?

I wormed my way through the crowd to a quieter hall on the left. It led to the principal's office and the dean of students' office I knew because I'd gone there first thing that morning to register. I stood in the hall, waiting for the crowd to thin out while I caught my breath. The wall on one side was lined with glass cases full of trophies. Separating the cases were notices about the different sports teams. There was a schedule for the boys' basketball league and a notice about cheerleaders' tryouts. Then I saw one that interested me: "Girls' soccer: We are thinking of forming a girls' soccer team. Anyone interested should show up on the soccer field, Thursday, January 2, at 3:30."

I pushed my way back into the stream of kids headed for last classes. My heart was beating wildly, not from nerves, but from excitement. They were forming a girls' soccer team. I remembered joining the soccer team in Birchington and Dee Dee inviting me to her party. Maybe I had finally found a way to belong after all! I could hardly wait until class was over and I could head for the soccer field.

Finally it was three-thirty. Arriving at the field, I noticed that the turnout didn't look very promising. It was clear that these girls lounging under a big tree were not like Dee Dee. In fact, they looked like a pretty scraggly bunch: some were too fat, some too tall, and none of them looked very athletic. When we started talking, I found out that most of them had never played soccer before. They looked at me as if I were their lifesaver. "You've played soccer before?" they asked excitedly. "On a team? That's great. You can coach."

"Carole will be so pleased to see you," a tall, skinny girl said. "She thought she was stuck with just us."

"Oh, I'm not that good," I said hastily.

"Wait till you see us play," the short, round one interrupted. "The trouble is that most of the athletic girls go out for basketball or cheerleading. It's hard to get girls to go out for soccer. Carole came from California where girls' soccer is really big, and she's determined to get a team going."

At that moment Carole came up, carrying a net of soccer balls. She looked like an Adidas commercial. "I had a terrible time getting these away from the boys' team," she said. "They didn't want to give us any, and I'm sure they all have leaks in them." She dropped them to the ground as one of the other girls introduced me, giving me a buildup I didn't deserve. Carole's eyes lit up. "Great—I'm really going to need help with this," she said. "They're not really big on girls' sports at this school, and they've never had a soccer team before. They still have the quaint idea that girls get all the exercise they need by being cheerleaders for the boys."

"They should have seen my team back in Massachusetts," I said. "We could take on almost any boys' team. We had girls who could kick the ball the length of the field."

Carole smiled. "Well, don't hope for that much here," she said. "But I'd sure like to show those boys we aren't hopeless. Let's get started, OK?"

"You have a nice field here, anyway," I said, helping her get the balls out of the bag. She looked up and laughed. "This is the boys' field," she said. "They'll be out in a minute after they've worked out with the weights in the gym. We get that dusty area over there behind the goalposts. See—it's the bit with the red plastic kiddie goals on it."

We made our way down to the girls' field and started. The girls weren't as clumsy as they looked, and the short, fat one, whose name was Cynthia, had a mean left foot. After we had done some drills, Carole suggested we have a scrimmage, seven against seven. That was really fun. It felt good to be playing a sport again, to be doing something I knew I could do well. I could see their admiration when I took the ball and dribbled it past the defenders.

We had been playing for about fifteen minutes when the boys' team came out. They were all dressed in uniforms and made a lot of noise as they ran out onto the field. But when they saw us, they all came over to watch, calling out a lot of loud, rude jokes. Their taunts were cruel and unfair, and I got madder by the moment. So, when the ball came near me again, I took it down the field. Skillfully dribbling it past all the girls who came at me, I whammed it into the goal. The boys on the sideline cheered.

"Hey, who are you?" one of them called as I jogged back to the center. "I haven't seen you around before."

"I'm Kristy, I just moved here," I yelled back. "And don't tell me who you guys are—I can guess. You're the cheerleaders for the girls' soccer team, right?"

The other girls laughed and yelled at my quip. In fact, I think it gave everyone the lift they needed. We played really hard for the rest of the game and showed the boys we meant business. When we walked off the field, dripping sweat, we felt pretty good. The boys stopped their workout to come over and talk.

"Hey, you guys didn't look half bad out there," one boy said.

"We don't intend to be half bad," Carole answered. "We have a star forward brought in from the East Coast."

I glanced up, embarrassed by all the eyes on me and found myself looking straight at Darren. Blushing twice as furiously as before, I searched desperately for the right words to say to him. He smiled and walked over to me. "I know this sounds corny, but haven't I seen you someplace before?" he asked. "You look really familiar."

"I don't think so," I said, praying he wouldn't remember the beach.

"Maybe it was at one of the parties over the holidays?" he asked.

"Maybe," I agreed.

"You really play soccer well," he said. "We thought it was a big joke when the girls wanted a team. But if they get as good as you are, we'd better watch out." His dark eyes held my gaze. I felt my knees weakening as if my whole body had turned to jelly.

"My name's Darren," he said.

I bit my tongue before I said, "Yes, I know." "Mine's Kristy," I blurted out instead.

"Would you like a ride home?" he asked me. "I have my bike outside, and we'll be done pretty soon."

"That sounds great. Thank you," I mumbled, still not completely in control of my tongue.

His smile broadened, and he gave me a wonderful wink. "See you by the locker rooms."

I don't think my feet touched the ground all the way back to the showers.

Chapter Twelve

"Hey, who was that gorgeous guy who gave you a ride home?" Ellen asked, appearing from nowhere as I waited for the elevator.

"Do you spend all your time waiting around the lobby to see who gives me rides?" I asked, joking. "Don't you have anything better to do?"

She sighed. "Yes, as a matter of fact. I have a twelve-page essay on the twentieth-century American novel to write, and I'll do anything to put off the dreadful moment when I have to start it. You wouldn't like to write it for me, would you?"

"You wouldn't want me to write it for you," I said. "It takes me half an hour to write two sentences."

"You're a lot of help," Ellen said. "And you

never answered my question. Who was the good-looking guy?"

I felt myself turning red again. "He's the one I told you about," I said. "The one I've been trying to meet, who looks like my boyfriend back home."

"But I thought he was real mean and yelled at you."

"He did," I said.

"And now he's changed his mind about you?"

"He didn't remember me," I said. "At least he didn't remember where he met me before. He was really nice today."

"You should watch it," Ellen said. "Guys with terrible tempers are not fun to be with."

"Oh, it's not like that," I said. "I understand why he yelled at me on the beach. He was about to be run down by a surfboard. He was scared and angry, and he yelled. I'd have done the same thing. You know, the way mothers yell at kids when they run out in the street? Anyway, it's different now. We're both on soccer teams, and we're meeting on equal terms." I smiled happily at the thought of it.

"Well, then good for you," Ellen said. "You're so lucky. About the most excitement I get at my school is when a stray dog wanders into a classroom! I guess I'd better go and get started on that essay. See you, Kristy."

The way she said "see you" reminded me a lot of Jason. He always said that, waving his hand lazily. *Now, why am I thinking about Jason when Darren is definitely interested in me?* I asked myself as the elevator rose slowly to our floor. *Why not think about Jason? After all, he's a nice person and a good friend.* It was comforting to know someone like Jason was around. Not that he had much time for me anymore. There always seemed to be a different, glamorous girl with him wherever he went. Still, I had the feeling I could depend on him if I really needed to.

The first couple of weeks at school were a lot less terrible than I'd thought they'd be. In fact, they went by quite smoothly. It made a big difference to know that there were people I could turn to. I had Jason at school and Ellen at home. And the girls from the soccer team had adopted me as a sort of guest star. They were always waving to me in the halls or inviting me to sit with them at lunch. I hadn't forgotten that Jason had also invited me to eat with him, but I kept seeing him with a miniskirted girl.

And then there was Darren. I saw him every day after school, and twice he gave me a ride home on his bike. Then one Friday night, after the boys had won their first soccer game of the season, I heard him running after me as I walked down the tiled hall toward the locker room.

"Hey, Kristy, wait up," his deep voice boomed.

I stopped, watching him come toward me with long, easy strides. He even ran like Don, with a wonderful fluid grace.

"Kristy, I wanted to ask you—" He stopped to catch his breath. "Are you doing anything tomorrow night?"

"Ah, nothing special, why?" I asked, smiling up at him. Trying hard to appear cool and mature, I was sure that somehow he could tell that my heart was already beginning to beat faster.

"Good, I'm looking for somebody to baby-sit my parakeet while I go out," he said seriously. But after one look at my disappointed face, he burst out laughing. "Just kidding," he said. "No, I really wondered if you'd like to go to that new club with me. It's got great music, and all the kids from school will be there."

"I'd love to," I said.

He smiled as if I'd made a wise choice. "Great," he said. "Pick you up around eight?" I nodded, and he strolled past me to the boys' locker rooms.

I spent most of the next day getting ready.

"Mom, she's in the bathroom again," Doug yelled.

I stuck my head out of the door. "Look, Douglas, I have a date tonight. He'll be here in half an hour, and my hair's still not dry. Now will you give me some peace?" I begged.

His face broke into a mischievous grin. "A date! Wowee! I'm going to write and tell Don."

"Go ahead," I said airily. "For one thing, your writing is so bad that he won't be able to read it.

116

And for another, Don wouldn't mind at all. He doesn't expect me to sit home and bite my fingernails, you know. Besides, he'd approve of this boyfriend."

He'd be flattered, I thought, putting the finishing touches on my makeup. He'd be glad that I chose someone just like him. It was fate that I met Darren.

I brushed my hair back from my face and looked at myself in the mirror. My skin looked golden brown against the white of my knit top. It was probably my own tan now, too, not the bottled one. And my hair, which had always been ash blond, had golden streaks in it. *Not half bad*, I told myself. All those hours in the sun playing soccer had been more than just good exercise.

Darren obviously thought so, too. "Not bad," he said, looking me over with a careful eye. "That outfit looks really good on you, Kristy." Then he led me outside to an old black car.

"I didn't think the bike would be a good idea tonight," he said. "So I borrowed my brother's car. It's a clunker, but it'll be more comfortable than the bike."

Luckily, I didn't have to worry about making conversation. Darren did a lot of talking. On the way through Honolulu, he told me all about his bike, how much he'd paid for it, and how he'd modified it for speed. He told me about surfing and the giant waves he'd ridden. I was just glad that he still hadn't associated me with the surfing accident. He was still describing how he'd won some competition against Australians and mainlanders when we pulled up outside an old warehouse. A flashing sign outside it said New Wave.

Once we got inside the club, conversation was impossible. The music was so loud that the walls seemed to throb with it. And the combination of music and the flashing lights made me dizzy. We found a group of Darren's friends in the corner and squeezed in next to them. I was introduced, but I couldn't hear anyone's name over the pounding of the music. Darren got us all drinks—a pinkish punch with lots of ice—then he held out his hand for me to dance with him. Whenever Don had touched my hand, I felt a tingle go right up my arm. Darren's hand didn't make me tingle at all.

Give it time, I told myself. *This is only your first date with Darren. You don't fall madly in love with anyone right away.*

Darren danced very well, moving unselfconsciously to the music. On the slow numbers he held me tightly, and I felt slightly uncomfortable being that close to him. At last the DJ took a break, and I sank back into my seat, resting my back against the cool stone of the wall. Darren and his friends were talking about people I didn't know. Then I heard one of them say, "Oh no, not him again." A young guy with a Hawaiian guitar came onto the stage, sat down and started to play. His songs were soft and mournful, in direct contrast to the pounding beat of the music that was playing before. He sang about lost loves, notes sent from one island to the next in bottles, and dreams that never came true. The songs weren't particularly original, but they were pretty, and the singer had a pleasant, deep voice.

Darren and his friends seemed to think the songs were very funny. They made loud comments to one another like, "Oh, here comes another song about the little birdies. How sweet!" When he sang "My Love Has Gone Now, Far Away," one of the guys yelled, "Good idea, why don't you follow her!" and the whole group laughed. I sat there, trapped in the corner, squirming with embarrassment. Finally, the poor guy finished and left the stage.

When the dancing started again, one of Darren's friends asked me to dance while Darren danced with a big, blond girl. I noticed he held her just as close as he had held me, and during the slowest number he actually whispered into her ear.

The club closed at midnight, and I was thankful to be going home. I hadn't felt comfortable all evening. I also had an uneasy feeling that these people would start talking about me as soon as my back was turned. In the darkness of the big car, I relaxed for the first time.

"Have fun?" Darren asked, putting an arm around my shoulder and pulling me toward him.

"Yes, thank you," I said politely.

"Good," he said. "That place is really the only fun spot in town. Most of the other clubs are full of Hawaiians, and they only play wimpy Hawaiian guitar music. They're way behind over here when it comes to music.

"Of course, they're way behind in most everything. Really primitive! I guess you haven't been here long enough to see yet, but their houses are horrible. They're full of babies and chickens and old men—it's like stepping into a 'National Geographic Special.' " He wrapped his hand around my shoulder and gave it a big squeeze. "You're so lucky that you met me on your first day at school," he said. "Now you're in with a group of mainland kids, so it'll be fine. You might have gotten yourself mixed up with some of these native kids—"

"Is that so bad?" I interrupted. I could feel myself trembling.

"Not bad, exactly, but boring. They're all a bit slow, if you know what I mean."

"So why do you stay here?" I asked.

He looked at me as if I was crazy. "My dad was posted here," he said. "I don't have any choice. Besides, where else is the surfing so great?"

We drove on in silence. I looked out the window.

"This isn't the way home, is it?" I asked, hearing my voice shake.

"Relax, I know this great lookout point," Darren said. "You can see the whole city."

"But I promised my folks I'd be in by twelve-thirty," I said, beginning to feel very uneasy. "They know the club closes at twelve. They'll start to worry."

"Hey, what's a few extra minutes," Darren said. "We're almost there. We'll take a peek at the view, then I'll drive you home."

A few minutes later the car glided to a halt. The view really was wonderful. I could see the ribbon of lights along the Waikiki waterfront and the twinkling stars in the dark sky above us. But I hardly had time to look before Darren pulled me into a bear hug. His lips were nuzzling at my neck. I turned my face away angrily. "What on earth do you think you're doing?" I asked.

"Oh, come on, Kristy. Just a little good night kiss," he said.

"Darren, stop it! I hardly know you," I insisted.

"But we were getting along so well, Kristy," he said. "Come on, don't be a little mama's girl. I'll have you home in time."

I wriggled away and huddled against the passenger door. "Did it ever occur to you that I don't want to kiss you?" I demanded.

My remark really surprised him. He drew back from me and stared out the window. "What's wrong with you?" he snapped.

"Nothing's wrong with me," I said. "But I have to feel something for a boy before I let him kiss me. And right now I don't feel a thing for you, except that I might hit you over the head any minute!"

He laughed uneasily.

"Are you going to drive me home, or am I going to have to get out and walk?" I shouted, my hand already on the door handle.

He looked confused. "I didn't mean to upset you. It's just that we were getting along so well before. I could tell you liked me. Why this sudden turn off?"

"Because I made a mistake," I said. "Now please drive me home." I could feel my voice wobbling. I was grasping the door handle with all my might. Then I saw headlights coming up the hill toward us. They turned off the road, and the car parked a little way down the hill from us.

It was just another couple up there to see the view. They wouldn't be any help at all. They'd probably think I was being as dumb as Darren did. Then the moon came out from behind the clouds, and I saw that it was an open sports car. I could see the moonlight shining on the driver's blond hair.

I was out of the door in an instant. "Jason!" I yelled. "Jason, is that you?"

He spun around, his mouth open in surprise. "Kristy?"

I ran toward him. "Oh, Jason. I'm so glad it's you."

He jumped out of the car and came over to me. "Kristy, what are you doing up here?" he asked in surprise.

"I came up here with Darren, and now he won't drive me home," I said. I was shivering even though the night was fairly warm.

I could see Jason's eyes, hard in the moonlight. "That was a dumb thing to do," he said. "Didn't it occur to you that it was pretty stupid to drive up here with someone you hardly know? And if I recall correctly, your first encounter with him wasn't exactly pleasant."

"I decided he was OK, and I didn't know we were coming here," I said, stung by Jason's fierce words. "I thought he was going to drive me home, and we came here instead."

He stared at me, frowning in anger. A tear welled up in the corner of my eye and escaped down my cheek before I could stop it. Jason's gaze softened. "Don't worry. I'll drive you home," he said. "You're OK now." He put his arms around me gently.

From Jason's car I heard a voice asking, "Jason? Jason? What's going on?" At the same time Darren climbed out of his car and came toward us.

"Kristy, what are you doing?" he shouted. "Look, I'll drive you home if you want." He ignored Jason completely.

"I'm driving her home," Jason said coldly. "So you can leave now."

Darren stepped up to Jason, glaring down at him. I noticed that Darren was much bigger and more muscular than Jason. "What business is it of yours, butting in like this?" he said. "We just had a little fight. We don't need your help."

Jason eyed him calmly. "Kristy asked for my help," he said. "Why don't you just go home?" He turned to me. "Come on, Kristy," he said, taking my elbow and steering me toward his car. "We're going home."

"Wait, Kristy," Darren called after me. "I don't want you getting in a car with a guy you hardly know."

"Oh, him?" I asked. "I wouldn't worry about him. He's just one of the wimpy Island boys you were telling me about. See you, Darren." I squeezed into Jason's car next to the girl in the miniskirt, and she glared at me all the way home.

Chapter Thirteen

Ellen was knocking on my door first thing the next morning. "So, how was the big date?" she asked. "I'm dying to know."

"It turned into a big disaster," I said. I sighed and poured two large orange juices, handing one to Ellen, who had followed me into the kitchen. "I hate to say this, but you were right. Just because Darren looks like Don doesn't mean he acts like him. He turned out to be the world's biggest creep."

"Why, what happened?" she asked, perching herself on the kitchen counter and sipping her orange juice. "He looked like such a hunk. I was sure you'd have a great time with him."

"There are other things besides looks," I said. "As I've now come to realize. First of all, he talked about himself the whole time, he had a crummy group of friends, and he flirted with all the other girls right in front of me. Then he drove me to some lookout point for a wrestling match."

"That's terrible," Ellen said. "What did you do?"

"I was really lucky," I said, realizing as I said it how very lucky I had been. "Jason drove into the next parking space and offered to take me home."

Ellen smiled. "You were lucky, but what was he doing up there in the first place?"

"He'd just pulled up to park with his girl-friend," I said. "I feel terrible about spoiling his evening. And she was so mad at me. But Jason didn't seem to mind. Anyway, I'm just glad he turned up. In fact, he's the only boy I'll ever talk to again. I'm giving up boys forever. I'm going to spend the rest of my life, sitting at home and learning to crochet."

Ellen smiled. "Gee, that's a shame. One of the reasons I came over—apart from being nosy about your date—was to invite you to a luau with me tonight. You haven't been to a luau yet, have you?"

I shook my head and said, "No, but I really don't—"

"This is the real thing," Ellen interrupted. "Not some tourist luau with a few bits of cold pig and a slice of pineapple. It's a real luau out at one of the houses in Makala—that's the rich part,

out past Diamond Head, ...
catering, and the daught...
school with me. You'd real...
be fun."

"I don't think so," I said. "...
face strange people again. No...

"But this'll be different," El... ...is is
family style. There'll be babies a... ...us and lots
to eat—and there should be some good Hawaiian
music. They're celebrating their great-grand-
parents' golden wedding, and half the island
will be there."

"But they won't want an outsider," I said.
Already I was wavering. I could tell that it would
be fun and also big enough so that I could be
invisible if I wanted to.

"Sure they will," Ellen said. "These things are
always open invitation. Everybody brings their
friends and relatives. And I told Karen, their
daughter, about you." She slipped down from
the counter again and put her glass in the sink.
"Besides," she added, looking over her shoulder,
"I get kind of scared in big gatherings, and I'd
really like to have a friend along to keep me company. Will you come—just to do me a favor?"

"OK," I agreed. "I'll come. Just as long as I
don't have to talk to any boys!"

One of the first things I noticed as we walked
through the huge brick gateway that evening
was that Ellen was not really scared of big gath-

ardly made our way around to the
nd the house when she started calling
etings to hundreds of people. She picked
babies and kissed them and hugged enormous old ladies dressed in flowered muumuus. I
was wearing a green and white sun dress with a
halter top and bare back. I'd been worried that it
was a bit too daring, but when I saw everyone's
outfits, I felt ordinary. Other girls my age looked
stunning in brightly colored strapless dresses or
wide Hawaiian print pants or jump suits.

"Here," Ellen said. "You need a flower to tuck
behind your ear." She put a big yellow hibiscus
into place. "Now you look perfect," she said.
"Come and meet Karen."

I looked out and saw that we were right above
the ocean, which was sparkling in the moonlight. Above the noisy laughter you could still
hear the crash of surf on rocks below. Miniature
lights were strung from enormous trees around
the wide rectangle of lawn. A long table, covered
in a gleaming white cloth, stretched for twenty
feet. It was piled high with salads, fruits, cold
meats, and pies. At one end of the table, smoke
was rising from the ground, carrying a delicious
smell toward us. And if that was not enough,
waitresses were carrying trays with glasses of
champagne for the adults, punch for the kids,
and enormous quantities of finger foods. Ellen
thrust a plate filled with miniature meat and
pineapple kebabs, stuffed tomatoes, and sweet

and sour meatballs into my hands. "To keep you going until the luau is ready," she said. "Oh, look, there's Karen and her family."

I was dragged over to a reception line and said a few polite words to a lot of people I didn't know. At the end stood a pretty girl who looked as if she belonged on a travel poster advertising Hawaii. We talked for a few minutes, until the next people in line wanted to talk to her. Then Ellen and I walked over and sat under a tree to eat the food.

"You'd better eat plenty now," Ellen warned. "They won't get around to serving dinner until ten at the earliest. I'll go and see if I can find us some more."

She was gone a long time. I sat invisible under the trees and watched the colorful procession of people laughing and talking as they passed. Everybody seemed to know everybody. Again I thought how wonderful it would be if I could belong somewhere like that. I wished I could be someplace with everyone who had known me since the day I was born.

Ellen came running up, panting, and thrust another plate into my hands. "Sorry it took so long," she said. "My uncle is short staffed tonight. He wants me to help him hand around stuff for a while. Do you want me to find you someone to talk to?"

"No, you go ahead," I said. "I'll be fine. It's fun to just watch."

"I'll be right back," she said, running off through the crowd again.

I watched a little while longer, but the pangs of homesickness for a place I'd never known became too strong. I walked through the trees and came out at a rock garden above the ocean. The moon had risen fully now and was casting silvery stripes across the calm water. In the garden down below, a guitar started playing, and women's voices started to sing in beautiful harmony. I sat down on a rock and gazed out to sea.

I don't know how long I sat there just looking and listening. After a while I heard footsteps crunching up the rocks behind me. I turned back, expecting to see Ellen coming to find me. Instead I came face to face with Jason.

"Oh," I said, scrambling to my feet. "I didn't expect to see you here."

He smiled. "I didn't expect to see you, either. Do you make a habit of perching yourself in remote spots, waiting for me?"

"I came up here because my friend had to help out with the food," I said. "It's so beautiful up here, isn't it? Like the end of the world." We stood there together, staring out across the ocean, listening to the roar and sigh of the waves. Then I remembered all the embarrassing details of the night before. I turned back to him. "Look, I'm really sorry about spoiling last night for you. I seem to wreck your day every time we meet. I'd better get back and find my friend. I'll leave you alone."

Jason put his hand on my arm. "Don't go, Kristy," he said. "Come and look at the ocean with me."

"I'd better be getting back," I said, feeling the warmth of his hand tingling all the way up my arm. "Ellen will be looking for me, and your girlfriend will be looking for you. She didn't think much of me last night, and I think she'd throw me into the ocean if she found me talking to you again."

Jason gazed down at me and smiled. "You're funny," he said.

"Oh, very funny," I answered, wishing he'd let go of my arm. For some reason it was making me confused. "I do the most amusing things, like causing a shark scare and hitting people with surfboards and interrupting dates—"

Jason continued to look at me. "You looked pretty sitting there with the moonlight shining on your hair," he said. "I was just thinking how boring everybody is—especially girls. All girls do is giggle and gossip and want you to go shopping with them."

"So you're giving up girls?" I asked lightly.

"The boring ones," he said. "I've decided that I need some excitement in my life. I need someone around me who yells about sharks and hits people with surfboards." He looked down. "I've been thinking about you a lot, Kristy," he said finally.

"You have?" I asked slowly.

"Yes, I have," he said in a low voice. "I found myself thinking about you when I was with other girls. Last night I was so angry when I found you up there with that creep! I realized how much I care about you. What I don't know is whether you care at all about me."

"It's funny," I said. "But I didn't think I did, except as a friend. I liked being with you, and I was glad that you were around, but that was all. At least, I thought that was all. I remember feeling jealous when I saw you with another girl and looking out for you around school. But when you put your arms around me last night, I knew it was more than that."

He leaned down and kissed me. His lips felt warm and gentle on mine.

"You know, we're both very dumb," he said as we drew apart again. "We were both looking for the right person when the right person was there all along."

I nodded, nestling my head onto his shoulder and shutting my eyes.

I was still sitting, wrapped in Jason's arms, when Ellen found us much later. "Oh, there you are," she said as I turned guiltily. "I came to tell you you'd better get down there quickly if you want any of the pig. They just got it out of the pit, and folks are eating as fast as they can carve." She didn't look at all surprised to see Jason's arm around my shoulder.

I stumbled to my feet. "I'm sorry, Ellen," I said. "I thought you were busy, and I had no idea we'd been away so long."

A broad grin crossed Ellen's face. "No need to apologize. I know when I'm not needed."

Jason got to his feet, too. "You're a terrific girl, Ellen," he said. "I'll remember you in my will."

She laughed. "Since you'll probably live to be a hundred like the rest of your crummy family, I won't hold my breath," she said.

I looked from one to the other. "You two know each other," I said.

Ellen nodded. "Of course we do. Everyone knows everyone else on these islands."

I started putting two and two together. "So all the time I was telling you about Jason, you knew who I was talking about?"

She nodded again. My suspicions were growing. "And you didn't, by any chance, invite me here tonight because you knew Jason was going to be here, did you?" I asked.

Jason squeezed me to him. "That was my idea," he said. "I take full blame. I thought about you all last night. I don't think it had ever crossed my mind before that you'd date other guys. I expected you to just be around. Dumb of me, huh? I realized last night that I didn't want to be with Sue or the other girls I know. They're nothing compared to you. I had to meet you and tell you, so I phoned Ellen first thing this morning."

"I'll say he did," Ellen said, punching his arm. "Eight o'clock on a Sunday morning! I was ready to kill him!"

"Who me?" Jason asked in mock horror. "After all I've done for you, Ellen Chan? Who rescued your sandwiches in kindergarten from that bully?"

Ellen giggled. "All right, I guess I owe you lots of favors—"

"And I am a warm and wonderful human being," he interrupted, holding me close to him.

"Oh, you're not bad, as boys go, is he, Kristy?" Ellen asked.

"As boys go," I said, turning my face up toward him, "he's not bad at all."

We were all laughing as we walked back toward the table.

Chapter Fourteen

That evening turned into one of the best in my whole life. I had never been around so many people who knew how to enjoy themselves before. People grabbed guitars and started singing, grabbed strangers and started dancing, and everywhere there was laughter. And since I was with Jason and Ellen, I was part of it, not an observer. I was right in the middle of everything, being grabbed to dance with some old grandfather or hugged by some aunt or having a little kid climb on my knee. And I could tell that everybody liked Jason, too. People called out to him wherever we went and wanted to meet me. And all the time they said the same thing, "He's a good boy, that one. He'll take good care of you."

By the time we got in the car to go home, I felt happier than I had in months.

"Have a good time?" Jason asked as I snuggled against him in the car.

"Wonderful."

"So did I," he said. "I had the best time I've had in years." He steered the car to a halt beside the ocean. "You know, Kristy," he said, staring out beyond me to the glittering water. "I think it must have been fate that knocked you into that flowerpot." Then he took me in his arms and kissed me. Again his kiss was warm and wonderful, but I remember forcing myself to think, *Hey, what about Don? Should I be feeling like this with someone else so soon?*

"Did anyone ever tell you you have the cutest little button of a nose?" Jason asked, interrupting my thoughts.

"I believe somebody did once," I said. "But he's a long way away."

"And you still think about him?" Jason asked. He looked at me earnestly.

"Sometimes," I said honestly.

"Then I'm going to keep you so occupied that you'll never have a minute to think about anyone besides me," he whispered, his lips lightly brushing mine again. "You won't believe it. We'll go surfing and snorkeling and dancing and to parties, and I'll follow you around at school like a shadow and take you to the spring prom in April and the picnic in June—"

"I thought you told me you always got tired of a girl after a few days," I said. I had to get the conversation lighthearted. I wasn't ready to have somebody plan so far ahead for me, especially since I didn't know what I wanted myself. All I knew right then was that I was happy to be with Jason and I really liked him. I didn't want to go one step farther than that, not even in my mind.

"That was other girls," he answered. "The boring ones. You won't ever be boring—"

"Oh, no," I said, laughing. "There are so many adventures waiting for me. I can fall off a wind surfer, meet an octopus when I'm snorkeling— all sorts of things."

He held me very close. "I won't let anything bad happen to you," he said. "Because I plan to keep you around."

"That's what you say now. What happens when a new miniskirt walks through the halls next week?"

He took my face in his hands, holding me very gently. "I realized something last night, Kristy," he said. "I realized that I was chasing a lot of girls because I wasn't ready for a real relationship. After I'd dated them a couple of times, I don't think I always got tired of them. I think I got scared that I might get involved. You see, I fell in love once. It was last year. I was crazy about her. Then one day she just showed up with somebody else. She didn't even tell me. I had no idea there was even anything wrong between us. That really hurt, Kristy. I didn't think I wanted to risk going through that again."

I felt a momentary stab of fear. *Oh, Jason*, I thought. *Can I be what you want me to be? I'm in the same position you were right now. I'm scared to get involved because it might hurt.* But I did want to be with him. I didn't want to pull back when he kissed me. I felt warm inside when he was close to me. Surely that was all anyone could ask or expect of a new relationship. I reached across and stroked his cheek, brushing back the blond curl that had flopped across his forehead. "Can we take it one day at a time, Jason?" I asked. "I have hurts to get over, too. But I promise I won't ever do anything behind your back, and we'll try never to hurt each other." Then we held each other very tightly and sat there, his cheek against mine, listening to the ocean roaring in the darkness.

It was very easy to slip into the routine of being Jason's girl. He'd call for me each morning, and we'd drive to school on his bike. He'd be waiting for me after class, and we'd leave school together, walking hand in hand down the hall. Being with Jason opened doors for me in school, too. I was Jason's girl, so I was included in everything.

After the first week, I watched for signs that Jason was getting tired of me. But I only had to see his face light up as I walked toward him to know that he wasn't. And I wasn't getting tired of him either. I enjoyed every minute I was with him. I had felt comfortable with him from the very beginning, and it was wonderful to know that I could always just be myself.

In fact, the one thing that spoiled our otherwise perfect time together was Don. I couldn't get him out of my mind. I didn't know if I ever wanted to forget about him. I still got letters from him every week, warm letters telling me all about school and his family and his job at the gas station. At the end of every letter he wrote that he missed me. I wrote back, too, telling him all about school, except that I didn't mention Jason. I wrote that I missed him, too, and sometimes I did. But I liked being with Jason, and it would have been perfect if I hadn't felt so horribly guilty about Don.

Not that I'm in love with Jason, I argued. *I really like him. That's all I can say right now.* Then I'd worry that Jason would fall in love with me, and I'd never feel the same about him.

If it sounds like I spent most of my time worrying and arguing with myself, it's not true. Most of the time I was with Jason, we just had fun. Almost everything we did together was fun. He took me over to meet his family. They lived in a big, rambling house, covered with creeping vines, that looked out over the ocean. The Whitmores were another of those big Hawaiian families with people coming and going all the time. And the whole bunch was ruled by a very fierce grandmother.

For some reason, the grandmother took a liking to me. Maybe it was because I beat her at checkers the first time we played. So I could do no wrong in her eyes.

"Kristy knows," she'd say to Jason. "She'll show you the right way to do that." I thought that Jason might be angry when his grandmother talked like that, but he thought it was wonderful.

As the weeks went by, I learned to surf fairly well and to wind surf as long as I went in one direction. The only way I could turn the board around was to fall in and then push it. Our soccer team won most of its games, and was even on the decoration committee for the spring prom. We'd planned, very ambitiously, to use only fresh flowers to decorate the auditorium. Somebody's uncle ran a huge nursery, and he was going to let us have all the imperfect flowers for nothing. We were also trying to borrow a working fountain.

Finally, Jason tracked down an indoor fountain at a bird sanctuary on the other side of the Island. The owner was, not surprisingly, a second cousin of Jason's, who agreed to lend it to us. One afternoon after school we drove over to see it. It was the first time I'd driven over the Pali, a sheer cliff where a Hawaiian king had driven his enemies to their deaths. We stood together by the railing and looked down. Below us, the mountain fell away to the plains. All around us peaks towered, as if pressing in on us, urging us over the edge. Black rock was everywhere. A big bird of prey soared out below us. Even though the weather was warm, I shivered. Jason slipped his arm around me. Then we climbed back into the car and started the long, winding descent to the bird sanctuary on the shore.

The fountain was just perfect—three stone basins, spilling down into one another with a musical splashing.

"I can see it's going to be a very high-class prom this year," Jason said as we walked back to the car. "No paper streams and balloons. Can you imagine how the hall will look strung with thousands of flowers?"

"I don't even know if I'll see it. I may not be going," I said, staring straight ahead of me as we climbed into the car.

"What do you mean?" he asked in surprise.

I smiled mischievously. "Nobody has asked me to go yet."

"Oh, I see. You need an official invitation," Jason said.

"Of course."

He turned and took my hand in his. "In which case, Miss Johnson, would you do me the honor of being my guest at the spring prom this year?"

"I'd be delighted, Mr. Whitmore," I said, and we both laughed.

"We're a couple of idiots, aren't we?" Jason said.

"Speak for yourself," I answered. "I'm perfectly sane."

"Not true. You have to be an idiot to spend so much time with me."

"Spending time with you is one of the things that proves how sane I am," I said.

"I'm glad you feel that way," Jason said, suddenly looking at me seriously and tenderly. Then he drew me toward him and kissed me, right there in the parking lot. And I didn't even care that other people might see us.

We got caught in a storm on the way home. Just as we reached the top of the Pali, the sky turned black, and rain fell on us in buckets. There was no time to get out of the car and put the top up. We just kept on driving, and by the time we came out of the little tunnel onto the Honolulu side of the mountain, the sun was shining again.

"I'll call you later," Jason said as he dropped me off. I climbed out of the car, kissed him lightly on the cheek, and ran up to the apartment.

"What happened to your hair?" Doug asked, looking up from a floor full of cars. "It looks terrible."

"You sure know how to flatter a girl," I said,

stepping between the cars. "If you must know, I got caught in a rainstorm on the Pali. Is Mom home?"

"She's down at the Chans learning how to make some sort of Chinese food," Doug said. Mom had been going down to the Chans a lot recently. Ellen's mother had taken her along on various volunteer projects, and they had become really good friends. Although she wouldn't admit it, not getting into the college courses had been the best thing that had ever happened to her.

"I'm going to take a shower before dinner," I said to Doug. "My clothes are all sticking to me."

"There's a letter for you on the table," he said, without looking up. "It's from Don!" Then he started chanting as he played. "Kristy and Don sitting in a tree. K-I-S-S-I-N-G!"

I went into my bedroom and shut the door. Little brothers could be pains. They always seemed to know how to say the right thing to make you mad. I threw Don's letter down on the bed and then went to take my shower. Mom put dinner on the table while I was drying my hair, so I didn't read the letter until much later.

"Dear Kristy," it began.

I'm writing instead of phoning with good news because I'm going to need to save every penny I can get. I've done so well at the gas station and made so much money that I don't have to wait to see you until summer vacation. I'm coming out for ten days over spring vacation instead! I'll bet you're surprised. I can imagine you falling off your chair as you read this! So get the camp cot out because I'm on my way. I can't really believe that I'll be seeing you again in two weeks. I can't wait to go swimming with you. I can't wait to be with you, period. It's been more than four months. Have you missed me as much as I've missed you?

Your one and only,
Don

Chapter Fifteen

I sat there, staring at his letter, for a long time. My mind was in a turmoil. I was thrilled that Don had missed me so much and that I was actually going to see him again. But he had ceased to be a real person in my mind. And now I was going to see him again. He was going to wrap real arms around me at the airport and kiss me with real lips. We could do all the things other couples did in Hawaii. We'd stroll along the ocean and watch the sunset under the palm trees. Maybe we'd take one of those catamaran cruises or drive up into the mountains.

I stared out of my window, across the blackness of the golf course, trying to picture myself and Don. The trouble was that Jason always slipped into all the scenes instead. I saw myself by the ocean with Jason, up in the hills with Jason. Even though Don was coming, how could I cut Jason out of my mind? Did I even want to?

I felt so confused. I longed to talk things out with somebody, but I couldn't think of anybody to turn to. Ellen would think I was letting Jason down if I welcomed Don. My parents probably wouldn't understand. After all, teenage romances weren't supposed to be *serious*.

"If only I knew what I wanted," I said aloud. "I do want to see Don again, I was really in love with Don. Maybe I still am in love with him. I can't stop him coming over anyway. He's saved up all that money for the fare. If only Jason understands."

That was the big problem. Would Jason understand? Would I understand if somebody said to me, 'I'm sorry but my old girlfriend is coming over for a few days, so you won't be seeing me until after she's gone.' I had a horrible feeling that things between Jason and me would never be the same again, and I was scared of losing him. But if I told Don not to come, then I'd lose him forever.

Suddenly I couldn't stand it any longer. I had to talk to Jason right away. I had to know that he understood and that it would be all right for Don to come. I rushed over to the phone.

"Jason," I said. "I have to see you right now."

"Is something the matter?" he asked urgently.

"I can't talk about it over the phone," I said.

"There's something I have to talk to you about right away. Can we meet somewhere?"

"I'll pick you up in a few minutes," he said. I heard the receiver slam down. I felt my heart hammering as I went down in the elevator to meet him. I had no idea what I was going to say or how he was going to react to it.

Maybe you're just blowing this whole thing out of proportion, I told myself.

Jason will understand, I kept telling myself as I stood there in the doorway. *We're more like brother and sister really. We have a good time together, that's all. We're not crazily in love with each other like Don and I were.*

Then my mind slipped into a daydream of Don. He was running toward me across the airport with his arms outstretched and his eyes glowing. I felt my stomach do its old familiar flip. *I do still love him*, I told myself. *He was my real love!*

At that moment the bike pulled up.

"So what's happening?" Jason called as I walked toward him.

"I can't talk here," I said. "Let's drive somewhere quiet."

He didn't argue but swerved out into the traffic. He pulled up at Queen's Surf, where the darkened park meets the beach.

Jason helped me from the bike. "Is this quiet enough?" he asked, attempting a smile. "Is the

147

CIA following us or something? Come on, what's so terrible that you can't talk about it at home?"

"It's not terrible," I said, walking ahead of him across the grass. I could hear the dead magnolia leaves crush under my feet. "It's just something I have to tell you. It's nothing bad, but I want you to understand."

"You're going to marry someone else," he quipped. "He's sixty years old and a millionaire!"

"Jason, please. Be serious and listen," I said. I turned back toward him. His fair hair shone in the darkness like a halo. He was looking at me with worried eyes. I perched myself on the edge of the seawall and stared out across the ocean. "You remember I told you," I began hesitantly, "that there was someone else back in Massachusetts."

"I remember," he said.

I took a deep breath. "I got a letter from him today. He's saved up enough money to come over and visit me. He's coming in two weeks."

There was a pause and then Jason said, "I see."

"He's only going to be staying for ten days," I said. "But I wanted you to understand why I wouldn't be around for a while."

"Oh, I understand," he said flatly. "You want to put me on the shelf until lover boy goes home again."

"Jason, it's not like that!" I begged. "I didn't

want to do anything behind your back. I can't keep him from coming—"

"No?" he interrupted. "It would be the easiest thing in the world to stop him from coming, if you wanted to. Just go home, pick up the phone, and say please don't come. That is, if you wanted to."

"That's just the point," I said. "I do want to see him again."

Jason said nothing for a moment. "Are you still in love with this guy?"

"I don't know," I said. "I really don't know. I have to see him again to find out."

"But you were in love with him once," he said. "I mean, really in love with him?"

"Yes, I was," I said.

He gave a big sigh. "Then that proves you can't be really in love with me, doesn't it? Because if you really loved me, you wouldn't want to hurt me like this."

"Jason, I don't want to hurt you," I said wearily. "I just want to see Don again, that's all. He'll be gone in ten days."

"Oh, sure," Jason said bitterly. "And then we can pick up where we left off, is that what you're saying?"

"I don't see why not."

"You don't see why not?" Jason yelled. "Do you think I'll want to hang around, knowing I'm only second best, thinking about you with someone else? Do you think I'll have fun when kids from school tell me they saw you with a strange guy, and I can say, 'Oh, that's her real boyfriend. I'm just the substitute over here.' "

"I don't think you're being fair, Jason," I said. "I have to sort things out for myself. Right now I don't know what I feel."

"I'll tell you what I feel," Jason said. "I've never felt about anybody in my life the way I feel about you. Right now I'm being torn apart. It's really a shock to realize you don't feel the same way about me. I always thought—" He broke off in a choked voice.

I reached out to touch his arm. He pulled back instantly. "I'd better drive you home," he said flatly. Then he turned and looked back at me. "I can't be second best, Kristy," he said. "I have too much pride, for one thing. And too much hurt. I guess I'd better stay out of your life from now on."

"I don't want to lose you, Jason," I pleaded.

"Sure you don't," he snapped. "It must be convenient to have your real boyfriend a few thousand miles away. You need some sucker here to drive you around and take you to the spring prom. That'll be while lover boy's here, by the way. I hope you don't have the nerve to bring him with you."

"Jason, don't," I said, feeling my eyes stinging with tears. "You're hurting me for no reason. I'm just asking you for time, that's all."

He didn't answer, but stalked ahead of me to

the bike. His feet angrily crunched through the dry leaves. He didn't say a word all the way home, and I didn't know what to say. I couldn't tell Don not to come, and yet I didn't want to lose Jason, either. His words still stung. He had no right to say such hurtful things to me. After all, I'd never told him that I loved him. We were friends, that was all. And friends shouldn't hurt each other that way.

The bike screeched to a halt outside my building. I slid awkwardly from the back of the bike. Jason didn't even get off. He sat there staring straight ahead of him.

"Please don't be mad at me," I said in a small voice. "I can't help it that I fell in love with someone before I met you."

Jason didn't stir. He sat like a statue on his bike, staring past me. Then he gunned the engine and roared away.

Chapter Sixteen

I watched Don's plane land, swooping down like a huge seabird and skimming in across the shimmering tarmac. As it turned to taxi toward the airport building, I tried to feel excited. *This is it*, I kept telling myself. *This is the moment you've been dreaming about for four months. Everything will be wonderful again.*

I had to keep on telling myself that, over and over, because I was finding it hard to believe. I knew Don was coming, and I wanted to see him again. I wanted us to have a wonderful time together. Everything would be just fine if only I could shake a picture out of my mind. It was Jason as I had seen him at school the day before. He'd been sitting out on the steps in front of school in deep shade. His arm was resting on the stone railing, and his chin was in his hand. He was staring out across the street, not seeing anyone who passed him. As I watched, someone called his name. He turned without smiling, shook his head, and got to his feet. Then he walked slowly off.

I felt at that moment as if someone had slapped me hard across the face. It had never occurred to me before that I had the power to hurt another human being. It had never occurred to me before that I had any power. I was the person who was picked up and dumped around the country every few years, who waited for other people to make friends with me, and who prayed one day I'd have a boyfriend like everyone else. My mother had told me that breaking up was one of the hardest things in life, but I never realized that I could be the one causing the pain. That was even harder to bear than my own pain.

I longed to run after him and beg him to forgive me, but I didn't know what to say to make things better. The only thing I could have told him to make everything all right again would be that Don was no longer coming and that I loved him best. And I couldn't do that without lying. I wanted to see Don again, and I did still love him. Those were the facts. If only life weren't so complicated! I remembered how much easier it had been before I'd gotten interested in boys. I'd made a few friends at school, played on a few sports teams, and then moved on. The friends and I had hugged one another and cried, then gradually we had forgotten. But every time I'd moved in those days, I'd come away with my heart in one piece. This time, it wasn't just being torn in two, it was being smashed into little pieces.

The plane had docked right below me. Baggage trucks were scurrying like beetles to the plane. There was no going back now. Don had come to see me, and I had to go meet him. I walked toward the gate. People were spilling out of the plane, talking excitedly. They were dressed in bright, vacation-style clothes, and they clutched straw hats. They all had pasty white skin, which did not compliment the bright colors of their shirts. Then Don came out. He was dressed in dark jeans and a gray velour shirt. But he was just as handsome as I remembered him. And he was much better looking than Darren was, now that I had the chance to compare them. I saw how much more interesting his face was than Darren's and how fine his cheekbones were. Don had an elegant face, an intelligent face. His dark eyes scanned the room. I found myself holding my breath in anticipation. He saw me, looked past, and then came back again. He broke into a run as I moved toward him.

"Kristy?" he asked, staring at me incredulously. "Is that really you?"

"Have I aged that much since you saw me last?" I asked, wondering what could be wrong with me. Was I really so ordinary that he'd forgotten what I looked like?

He dropped his bag and took my hands in his. "Not aged, changed," he said. "I hardly recognized you. The blond hair and the tan. You look like you've lived here forever."

"Is that bad?" I asked, surprised that I could have changed that much.

He smiled, his gorgeous, sparkling smile. "No, it's wonderful," he said. "You look like something off a travel poster."

"That's funny," I said. "That's what I thought about all the other girls when I first arrived. I hadn't realized I'd been in the sun so much. But I suppose with soccer practice and riding around on the bike all the time—"

"Bike? You've taken up bicycling?" he asked.

Mistake number one. "Oh, no, just a friend who gives me a ride to school on a motorbike," I said. "They're popular here."

"I can see why," he said. "But at home your hands would freeze to the handlebars half the year."

Why are we standing here making this polite conversation? I asked myself. *We'll be talking about the weather next.*

"And how is the weather here?" Don asked. "We've had such a bad winter. There are places at home that still have snow."

155

"Really?" I managed politely. "The weather's fine here. It's always just the same. Sun every day and a shower every now and then."

Don wrinkled his nose. "How boring," he said. "Don't you long for those cool, crisp days with a wind blowing or a gentle spring rain? It must be terrible to have only one season."

No, I said to myself in surprise. *I certainly wouldn't want cold winds blowing.* Looking at Don, I said, "I'd find it really hard to go back to winters again after this."

"I'm a winter person myself," Don said. "I remember telling you that once. It was on the ice rink before you left. Do you remember, Kristy?"

"Yes, I remember," I said. "You were wearing your red scarf. You towed me around so fast. I've thought about it often, like replaying a movie."

His face softened, and he looked down at me tenderly. "Have you?" he asked. "I've thought about you often, too. I'm glad you've missed me."

Then he took my chin in his hands and kissed me gently on the lips. "Oh," I said, laughing. "Your lips are so cold!"

He laughed, too. "They pressurize those planes," he said. "I had the blanket wrapped around me all the way here. I'll warm up soon, and then I'll give you a decent hello."

He picked up his bag and took my hand. "Let's go find my suitcase," he said. "And see if they've sent it to Florida instead!"

We arrived home in time for dinner.

"Wow, it looks like you live in a hotel," he said, eyeing the tall building and the uniformed doorman. "Does everyone live like this over here?"

"Oh, we're just living here until we can find a house somewhere," I said. "There isn't that much that we can afford that's close enough to the city."

"Who'd want to move when you live in luxury like this?" Don asked, looking around the marble entrance hall.

"I miss having our own furniture," I said. "It only arrived last month, and it's been sitting in storage since then."

While we were waiting for the elevator, Terry Chan ran through the lobby, yelled something to our doorman, and bounded up the stairs. Then old Mrs. Minagawa crossed the lobby, calling out a greeting as she passed. Don raised his eyebrows but didn't say anything. Once we were safely inside the elevator, though, he looked at me. "It's like living in the United Nations," he said, shaking his head.

"Our neighbors are all very nice. Mom has never made so many friends as she has here."

"Amazing," Don said.

My family gave Don a tremendous welcome, and my mother had really gone crazy making a special Hawaiian dinner. We started off with papaya and mango salad. Then we had spareribs with pineapple and fried Chinese noodles. It was Mrs. Chan's special recipe. Don claimed he wasn't very hungry after the long flight, and we finished the extra food for him easily.

After dinner we had cold drinks out on the *lanai*. Don sank down onto the chaise longue, mopping at his forehead.

"Pfew," he said. "Doesn't it even cool down at night here?"

"Not very much," I said. "I guess we just don't notice the heat anymore. We felt it at first." I sat down beside him and leaned back with a contented sigh. "I'm so full," I said. "You should have eaten your share, so I wouldn't have been tempted to make such a pig of myself. Wasn't that a terrific meal?"

"Oh, sure," he answered uneasily. Then he asked hesitantly, "By the way, what was all that stuff?"

"The food, you mean?" I asked in surprise. "The salad was mango and papaya."

"What are they?"

"They're fruits. They grow here. And Mom cooked the ribs and noodles Chinese style. Mrs. Chan has been teaching Mom. She's a great cook. You should see the way she does a whole fish in paper. It just melts in your mouth."

"So you go in for that sort of food a lot now, huh?" Don asked. "I suppose regular food is hard to get here?"

I laughed. "Not really," I said. "If you walk two blocks from here you'll pass a McDonalds, a Jack-in-the-Box, a Wendy's, a Kentucky Fried

Chicken, and just about every other fast-food place you've ever seen."

"Great," he said. "Then I won't starve." He reached out and put his arm around me. "So tell me about everything that's happened to you since you left Birchington," he said.

Everything I wanted to tell would have to have Jason censored out of it. "You tell me about you first," I said. "I'm dying to hear about everybody and what they've been doing."

"Well," he said, "really not too much has happened. Our basketball team came in third in the big tournament, and Robbie was named outstanding player. He's broken up with Jeanie, by the way. She's going with Tod Patterson now. And Dee Dee's going with my cousin, Hal. His father, my uncle, has started developing that land beyond the shopping center. He's going to put condominiums on it, and everyone in town is going crazy. They've had a town meeting about it, but, of course, my uncle has connections in city hall, so they didn't get too far!"

"And what about you?" I asked. I felt bewildered by all the names I hadn't thought about in months. "What have you been doing?"

"We had the football awards banquet in January," he said. "It was such a riot. There were some guys waiting outside for us, and when we came out, wearing our best clothes, they pelted us with snowballs. Of course, we wouldn't let them get away with that. We chased after them, and there was a free-for-all. You've never seen so many wet suits in your life!"

"And what about college?" I asked. "Have you been accepted anywhere yet?"

"I found out the day before I left that I've gotten into Boston University. My cousin's still there, and my uncle went there, too. And after college I'm going to work with my uncle. He's told me the job's waiting for me, which is nice to know."

I stared out into the black velvet night. I tried to imagine what it would be like to know that my future was planned out for me, even after college. It was a scary thought. Now completely warmed up, Don had launched into a description of how his father was remodeling the old greenhouse. Don made it sound like a very important undertaking. I was trying to listen when I heard a motorbike on the street below us. It slowed down and then speeded up again.

"Oh, I'm sorry. What did you say?" I asked, realizing that I hadn't been listening.

Don smiled. "No wonder you can't hear," he said. "It certainly is noisy out here. Maybe we'd better go inside."

"Sure," I said, wanting to please him.

After he'd finally gone to bed, I took a good look at myself in the mirror. I hadn't noticed any big change before, but looking at myself objectively, I could see that I did look different. My hair had been bleached almost totally blond by the sun. The front wisps were almost white. It had grown a lot in four months and curled around my shoulders, heavier and fuller after lots of contact with ocean water. My face was very tan, which made my normally blue-green eyes look completely blue. *They're just like Jason's eyes*, I thought. Quickly I made myself blot out the image that came into my mind.

I was busy the next few days showing Don all the sights. He had a good time, but it annoyed me that he treated the whole thing like a huge joke, as if he were visiting a zoo. "So this is history, Hawaiian style," he'd say when I showed him the old queen's palace. He thought the children were cute and the adults quaint. I took him to the beach one day, and he got a terrible sunburn, which made spending any more time in the sun impossible. Not that he liked the beach very much anyway. He told me he didn't like the feeling of sand between his toes and showered for a good ten minutes afterward.

But I did persuade him to overcome his fear of beaches long enough to go with me to Hanauma Bay. After all, it's not everywhere you can swim in an aquarium! There again I was surprised at how far I had come in such a short time. I, who had hardly dared put my face in the water, was showing Don how to use a mask and snorkel. I couldn't help laughing as he lowered his head cautiously into the water. We swam out into the deeper water, but I had to stop and wait every few yards for him to catch up or adjust his mask.

However hard I tried, I couldn't stop seeing an image of Jason, sleek as a fish, skimming along under the water with no apparent movement.

"Kristy, wait." Don grabbed at my arm.

"What's wrong?" I asked.

"There's a snake down there!" he said, peering down anxiously.

"Oh, that's only an eel," I said. "It won't hurt you."

"Did you always swim this well?" Don asked grouchily. "I'm having a hard time keeping up with you."

"I've had a lot of practice recently," I said.

"Well, I suppose there's nothing else to do around here," he agreed.

"We'd better get back to the shore, or your back will burn again," I said, feeling angry at myself and at him. Why did he have to insult everything he saw? After all, Birchington, Massachusetts, was not so hot when it came to entertainment! One movie theater and the Birchington Players production of *Arsenic and Old Lace* was hardly major excitement. I almost said that out loud, but then I remembered that Don was just in Hawaii for a little while. He had saved up all that money to come and see me, and I knew I should try to be understanding.

Only a few more days, I found myself thinking. I was shocked at myself.

As we were lying on the beach drying off, a

boy came up to me. It was Tiny, one of Jason's friends.

"What's happening about the fountain, Kristy?" he asked. "Are we getting it for the dance?"

"I don't know, Tiny," I said. "You'll have to ask Jason. I'm not doing the decorations anymore. I won't be going."

His face fell. "Oh, that's too bad," he said before I could stop him. "Did you and Jason split? That would explain why he's going around growling at everybody."

"Yes. Well, I have to be going, Tiny," I said. "Have a good time Saturday." I grabbed my towel and started up the beach before he could say anything else.

On the bus on the way back, Don was very quiet. He was quiet all the way up the boulevard back to our apartment. Then as we stood under a huge magnolia, waiting to cross the street, he said suddenly, "It's no good, is it?"

"What isn't?" I asked, looking up at his face.

"Us, I mean," he said. "We've been trying to make it work, but something's missing. I don't fit in here, and you fit in too well. It's like you're on a different planet from me, Kristy."

"I know," I said. "I've been feeling the same way. Back in Massachusetts, you were the one who belonged. And I enjoyed belonging by being with you. But now it's like we're talking different languages."

"And I get the feeling that's not all that's come between us," he said. "There have been too many times you've started to tell me something and stopped in the middle. I get the feeling that you've met someone you care about more than me. Am I right?"

"Yes," I said, looking up at him openly. "I didn't think I had. I thought he was only a friend. But I've been trying to get along without him for almost two weeks now, and I can't."

"And you're not going to a dance on Saturday because of me?" Don asked gently.

I nodded.

He smiled. "I think I'd better see if the airline can find an earlier flight for me, don't you?"

"But you came all this way, Don," I said. "I don't want to spoil your vacation."

His smile broadened. "Well, I've seen Hawaii, which is more than anyone else in Birchington. And I'll be the only person in town with a tan this early." He reached out and took my hand. "I don't want to interrupt your life, Kristy," he said. "After all, it looks like you belong over here now, and I belong back there."

"Hey, you going to move?" an old woman said from behind us. She was prodding us in the backs and pointing to the pedestrian light, which had changed to green. We stepped out into the sunlight and hurried across the street.

Chapter Seventeen

I saw Don off at the airport the next afternoon.

"I feel so bad that you didn't have a good time here," I said. "And that I wasn't what you wanted me to be."

He put his hand gently on my shoulder. "Don't feel bad," he said. "People change. We were right for each other back home, and we're not right here. It's as simple as that. We didn't promise to love each other for the rest of our lives, you know."

"I know," I said, smiling. "But I honestly didn't know how I felt about Jason until I had to give him up."

"That's often how it happens," Don said. "The thing we want is right under our noses, and we don't recognize it until it's too late."

"How come you're so wise?" I asked, looking up at him and noticing again how deep and serious those brown eyes were.

"I guess I'm just a warm and wonderful human being," he said, smiling.

"You really are," I said. "And I'll treasure the time we had together all my life. When I'm old and gray, I'll say to my grandchildren, 'He was my first boyfriend, and he was very special.' "

Don put his hands on my shoulders. "Let's try not to have an emotional scene, OK?" he said. "I don't want both of us sobbing in the middle of an airport! Everyone will think that I'm a rat and I'm deserting you."

"All right. No more emotional scenes," I said. "I want you to go home thinking good thoughts about Hawaii. It's a wonderful place."

"It's certainly beautiful," he agreed. "But I don't think I could ever live here. I'd feel like I was at Disney World all the time."

"I did at first," I said. "But I got over it when I made friends and could escape from the tourists."

"That reminds me," Don said. "Will you still be able to get a ticket for the junior prom? I hope I haven't spoiled that for you."

"I don't know," I said hesitantly. "I don't even know if Jason will want to go with me now. He was pretty broken up when I told him about you. And he has a lot of pride. He might not want me back now."

"Do you want him back?" Don asked.

"Yes," I said. "I want him back terribly."

"Then go tell him that," he said. "It sounds like an offer no man could refuse."

The last boarding call crackled through the waiting lounge. There was a rush for the gate.

"I'd better go," Don said. "Goodbye, Kristy."

"Goodbye, Don—and good luck in everything. I'll visit Birchington ten years from now, and you'll be another Partridge settled happily there, maybe even mayor!"

He laughed. "Probably," he said. "And you'll have lived in ten more states and be a sophisticated world traveler."

"I don't know about that," I said. "They're going to have a hard time dragging me away from here."

"I'm glad you've found a place you really like, Kristy," Don said. "Enjoy yourself, OK?" He took my chin in his hands again and kissed me gently. I felt his lips warm and tender, but there was no more tingle. He was just a very nice person who was going home.

I didn't wait to watch his plane take off. I sped home and borrowed Ellen's bike, heading out toward Jason's house. I had no idea what I was going to say, but somehow I was going to make him listen.

I was scared to go up and ring the front door bell. His family might just tell me to go away, and I didn't want to face Jason himself standing on

167

the doorstep. I saw that his bike and the red car were both in the driveway, so I knew he had to be around somewhere. Then a gardener walked past and said that Mr. Jason was "out back someplace."

I walked around to the back of the house and heard the sounds of a guitar coming from under the big banyan tree. He was sitting with his back against its enormous trunk, almost hidden by its tangle of roots and branches. He didn't see me come toward him, and he didn't hear me because of the guitar. I ducked beneath an aerial root and squatted down beside him.

"Hi," I said.

He glared at me suspiciously. His hand rested on the ground giving him the look of an animal poised to run away. "What do you want?" he asked.

"I thought you might need some help fetching fountains," I said.

He continued to stare at me as if trying to read my mind. "What about lover boy?" he asked in a quiet voice. "Are you volunteering his help as well?"

"Don has gone home," I said.

His look softened. "What happened? Did you have a fight?"

"We both realized that there was no point in his staying any longer," I said evenly, "when all the time I was thinking about someone else."

"You were thinking about someone else?"